Hard Lovin' Straight Thuggin'
A Southside Love
Written by: S. Yvonne

Other Books By S.Yvonne

Chapter 1

Messiah (Gu) Carter

"Young ain't no buster, never said I was a saint, never said I was an usher, so how ya'll gon' sit and tell me I ain't no hustler, I got bitches all around me, young like Usher, don't leave your bitch around me, young might fuck her."

Jeezy blast through the sound system in my tricked out Camaro, while I rode through the hood bobbing my head to the music; rapping along with the lyrics, I felt like the man of the year thinking about all the money I'd just counted up in my safe an hour before. Looking to the right of me my lil piece RaRa sat there in her bag, complaining as usual. RaRa was pretty as hell with cinnamon skin, nice toned body with a medium frame, wide hips and ass. Her lips were pink and full, and she wore her hair cut completely off in a strawberry colored brush cut that complimented her long lashes and natural grey eyes. Baby was sexy as fuck, hands down, but I couldn't stand a complaining ass female and she didn't seem to get that shit. We'd been kickin' it for a year and she still didn't know how to treat a nigga like me. I didn't understand it, I gave her everything she wanted and all I needed her to do was keep it 'G'... stand by a nigga side and don't give his pussy away. Don't complain when I was getting money, especially when it was getting spent on her ass too, cook a nigga a hot meal and stop tryna stuff me with oodles and noodles and shit, hell, do some productive shit... anything... just stay off my back.

"You don't think a nigga wanna see you a lil more than what I do RaRa?" I drove using my knee to steer the wheel so I could roll my joint. "On the real, we pose to be chillin' and you crabbin' for no reason. I been busy Ra... act like you know what it is man, you trippin'." The past year had been rough as fuck for a young nigga like me having my ups and downs from fast money to slow money, old tricks to new tricks, dusty bitches to bad bitches, fake niggas and real niggas, baby mama drama to.... Nah scratch that part; just throw the whole baby mama away... I don't even wanna think about that bitch. Point is, a nigga had it rough in the hood and out here in these streets at twenty-two I was lucky to still be here, shit, matter fact I was on my Drake shit right now.... I needed a moment of silence cause NIGGA I MADE!

Ra sucked her teeth and gently grabbed the joint from my lap, "here, let me do it before you fuck around and kill us."

"Give it back, I'm straight."

She ignored me and pulled the wrap up to her lips anyway, carefully tucking the weed inside making sure not to let it fall out. "I said I got it!"

"Don't get all that sticky ass lip gloss all over my shit Ra, I'm serious yo... that shit fucks with my mental when I'm tryna get high."

"I said I got it, the light is green, nigga go..." she waved me off with one hand while I watched that one crease in the middle of her forehead that showed up every time she was trying to focus. "I'm just saying, you need to do better Gu..."

"I'm tryin' ma... damn."

"What you getting frustrated for then?"

I sighed and tried my hardest not to get mad, "You already know the answer, just stop nagging me and shit and we gon' be good, trust me."

Ra chuckled but I didn't see what the fuck was funny, this shit here was aggy and if I wanted to deal with it I could've stayed with my baby mother. Speaking of baby mother I thought her ass right on up as her calling interrupted my music with her name showing up through the dash screen from the Bluetooth. I gave RaRa a look and she knew what time it was. Rolling her eyes, she sighed and shook her head, "go ahead."

Pressing the answer button, I spoke right in front of Ra as Hennessy's voice blasted through the speaker. "Gu? I know you there... why didn't you come personally bring me my money? Like, why do we have to play these games? I shouldn't have to pick up money orders from yo mama's house when you're very capable of giving it to me yourself."

Just like I thought, all she wanted to do was call a nigga and argue all the damn time and I didn't have time for that shit. "Nessy, I don't have time for this shit tonight. Why the fuck does it matter where you have to get it from? If you wanna see a nigga just say that but don't be callin' me with the bullshit man. Matter fact, I can't even do this shit right now..."

"Where you at Gu?" She asked.

"In the car... driving." I answered feeling Ra burning a hole through the side of my face. "And that's another reason why I gotta go... how many times I gotta tell you I don't like arguin' and especially when I'm drivin', I need to be focused."

"Fuck that Gu! I'm tired of playing these games with you!"

Silence.

"Gu?!"

Silence.

"Gu?! Stop fucking playing with me, I know you're there. Your daughter wants to speak to you."

Silence.

"G-... Gu?" She lowered her voice.

"See what I'm talking about Nessy? Nigga just got into an accident fuckin' round with yo ass man!"

She gasped, "Oh my God Gu are you serious? I'm sorry, where you at?" She asked sounding like she hopped straight up out the bed; hearing her keys dangling in the background I really wanted to laugh... that'll teach her ass.

"Nessy, sit down somewhere crazy ass girl, I'm aiight man I ain't get into no accident but you get my point right? Now chill..."

"You know what? FUCK YOU MESSIAH! That shit ain't even funny, and since we being so petty I want my money doubled next week!"

Click!

"What's wrong with you?" I asked Ra already knowing the answer.

She folded both her arms across her chest and chuckled again, "nothing Gu... park on 1st street, I wanna run in my auntie's apartment to grab some stuff.... Damn, why all these police here?"

I pulled up to the hood with every intention on hollerin' at my rounds just as soon as I was finished rolling up but what RaRa had just implied had my attention. It wasn't like it was unusual to see the police around the hood but this shit looked a lil deeper as my eyes zoomed in on the yellow tape, which meant somebody somewhere got murked. I sat my joint in the side of the door. "Hurry up RaRa... shit look like they in front of my ole girl crib."

The screeching sounds of a woman screaming caught my attention. "RONNIEEEEE! THAT'S MY BABY! THAT'S MY BABY! NOOOOO!" I think my legs registered before my brain did. I tuck my chain in my black Polo and took off toward the screams and reached my mama just as she was trying to fight the police through the crowd not giving a fuck about them trying to stop her, she beat on the officer's chest. "You motherfuckers let them kill my boy! They killed my boy!"

"Sue!" I grabbed my mama tryna get her to look at me. "Everybody back the fuck up, damn give a nigga some room! The fuck, ya'll see me tryna calm her the fuck down!" I snapped pulling her from the officer with my eyes affixed on the bloody white sheet covering the lifeless body in the road. "Sue! Mama!"

"If you don't refrain her we're gonna have to do so." The long face blonde head officer warned.

I shot his ass one more look hoping that he got the picture cause I didn't give a fuck about no police. This was the part of Miami these muthafuckas tried to stay away from anyway. They didn't give a fuck about us out here in 'Da Nolia'. With a nod of the head, he backed away to tend to the rest of the residents of 'Da No'. I placed Sue's head into my hurting chest cause I knew that my lil cousin Ronnie was gone. I hadn't found out what happen but I was gonna get to the bottom of this shit. Ronnie had just turned eighteen but he wasn't Sue's biological son... she only had me at the time and then a couple of years later, my sixteen year old sister 'Bari' came along. My mama's sister Becka used to be wildin' back in the day when she had Ronnie but when DCF showed up on the doorstep to take Ronnie away from Becka at one years old, Sue wasn't having it and she took on the responsibility of raising Ronnie on her own although she was twenty with her own responsibilities. *'Becka!'* She told my auntie back then, *'I will not let these white folks come up in here and put my nephew in the system! You need to get yo shit together and keep yo fuckin' legs close if you can't handle this mommy shit!'*

Auntie Becka, who was the replica of Sue, didn't give a fuck anyway cause at 17 years old running the streets was what she wanted to do without being tied down to a little ass baby that depended on her to do everything. Although Sue and Becka were only three years apart, let my granna tell it, Sue was always the mature one. They both were a pretty dark skin the color of smooth Hershey chocolate with a decent grate of hair since my granna was half black and Indian, and my granddaddy was from the little island of Turks and Caicos. They had plenty fights in Da Nolia housing projects with random bitches over the years all because half the hoes was mad that they baby father's wanted a feel off Sue and Becka, whom were still two of the baddest women walking 'Da No'. I think that was a part of the reason I had never left the nest and what I mean by nest, I mean these stomping grounds. I had my own apartment right across the street but I myself had never left here. Shit, if they didn't do it, why should I have had to?

I remember plenty days we didn't even have a meal to eat but Sue got out there and hustled no matter if it was selling pussy or selling pills, she made shit happen. Every holiday there was a miracle on the table and the lights nor water never got cut off. We were one of the poorest in the hood but Sue still made sure she stole us all the flyest shit. It was me who taught Ronnie's little bad ass how to tie his shoe, or ride a bike without training wheels. Hell, since neither one of our mama's had insurance to get us circumcision surgery when we were born, it was me who explained to Ronnie how to take care of his pullback to make sure he stayed on point' especially since I'd learned how to handle my oversized dick at a young age. When I started getting money, I paid for Ronnie and me both to go have the procedure of circumcision done and we suffered that pain together after that. Ronnie grew all the way up though, and he let the niggas from the other side get in his head. I told him over and over to stay away from them jealous ass Overtown niggas cause that shit could only bring him trouble. Besides, he wasn't a street nigga anyway. Ronnie was suppose to go away to college and do something with himself. I sheltered his ass as much as I could but me doing that only made him wanna get out there even more.

Now he was filled up with bullets and never coming back, that shit cut deep as I tried to stifle the tears from falling. I pressed Sue's wild haired head into my chest and closed my eyes, "it's gon' be okay mama... I'mma find out who did this."

She gripped a handful of my grey Saint Laurent hoodie and looked into my eyes, the same exact brown of hers with the same long ass female lashes that I hated. Looked good on her but was a no go for me although all the broads loved it. "You better handle this shit.. you hear me! Handle it son." She let me go and broke through the crowd disappearing as everyone got the fuck outta her way.

I frowned scolding the many faces of the hood that I'd been looking at for years and asked, "so nobody don't know nothing huh?" I clench my jaws. They knew not to fuck with me... period. Nobody wanted to feel the raft of Gu when I got mad and started terrorizing shit. Everybody backed away and scattered not wanting to get me riled up.

"Messiah!" I looked to the right of me to see Bari's lil cream colored face pushing through the crowd with her best friend Bambi not too far behind her. I frowned noticing the makeup on her face but now wasn't the time to address it although I made a mental note to address that shit later. Bari knew how I felt about her and she knew how I felt about her wearing that shit on her face drawing more attention to her already pretty face and perfect frame. Standing at 5'2, 135 pounds with a round face, wide hips and small round behind, Bari was a beautiful slim thick and I hated it. I swore if one of these fuck niggas from around the way even touched her I was pressin' bout my little sister. She wouldn't be getting' no dick until she turned 40 years old if I had anything to do with it. "Messiah!" She finally made it to me with her arms fold in front of her chest with visible tears in her eyes. "What happen to Ronnie?!"

I gently push her away from the yellow tape not wanting her to even see it, "let me holla at you Bari..." she didn't oblige.

"Hold up!" Bambi came rushing behind us with her ghetto fabulous ass wearing a short red romper and the matching red Huarache's. Bambi was known around the hood ass 'legs' since she had some nice ass brown legs. She wore red lipstick on her full lips and her hair in a long ponytail not looking her age at all. A lot of niggas in the hood wanted to touch her lil ass but honestly, if she was of age, I still wouldn't smack her with no dick outta respect for her being Bari's best friend. "Don't leave me out here, shit I'm coming too."

I paused and looked at her briefly before making a decision, "come on man... damn." The warm humid air smacked my face causing me to remove my hoodie and expose my ripped physique and tattooed arms before addressing the issue. "Bari." I placed both my hands on her shoulders and looked into her eyes. "Who was all out here? That's all I need to know."

She dropped her eyes and wiped a tear, "even if I knew, I still wouldn't tell you. I don't want you to get killed too Messiah." She mumbled, she was the only person who could get away with calling me that shit.

Bari was always over sensitive but now wasn't the time for that, "Bari, I'm good... I need to know if you was out here, tell me."

Silence.

I was getting real damn agitated and Bambi could tell so she boldly stepped in front of Bari like she was guarding her or something. With both her hands on her hips she told me straight up, "you know those chicks that live in the back?" She asked. "The chick Turquoise who lives in the back with her older sister or whoever that is?"

I balled my lips, "what's up Bam? You got something to say then say it ma... that's my cousin laying out there on the ground."

"I understand and I got you, shit, between you and I... Ronnie and I had a lil thing a few times. He's the one that turned me on to womanhood if you know what I mean." For whatever odd reason, I wasn't even surprised knowing Bambi was fast and if Bari even tried it I was gonna break her fucking neck. "But anyway, Turquoise been out on the stoop all day and I know she had to see something."

That name didn't ring a bell, "I don't know her."

"She's new around here, she ain't been around too long. There she goes right there." She pointed at a brown skin thick chick rocking some faux locks with a very exotic look about her. Noticing us staring at her, she disappeared looking uneasy and back into the crowd.

I stroked the perfect trim of my goatee and nod my head trying to fight back the tears, "aiight... bet! Ya'll go inside for the night, shit too hot out here... and Bari, Sue needs you... she goin' through it. Becka should be on her way back to the hood so just hold them down for me."

Bari wiped her tears and grabbed Bambi by the hand, Bambi looked back and gave me a sympathetic look before disappearing. I made my way back to the front with my gun tucked just in case a nigga wanted to get cocky, especially since I don't know where the bullets that killed Ronnie came from... I was looking at everybody side eyed. My people were off limits, period! The whole time I was walking, everybody was looking at me feeling sorry and shit, but I wasn't gon' break in front of nobody no matter what. I couldn't wait till the police left cause I wanted to paint the fuckin' city red tonight.

~~~~~~

Knock! Knock! Knock!

"Messiah! Open the door!" Hennessy demanded waking me up out my sleep. I struggled to open my eyes with my head throbbing and a badass headache. After finding out about Ronnie's death last night, shit really fucked with me and make it so bad, twelve stayed on the block all night investigating just to come up empty cause wasn't nobody in 'Da Nolia' giving up no info, and since they were out so long... I couldn't even do my own, which had me more than pressed. I turned it in for the night but I didn't even remember passing out. Looking around at the many of empty Heineken bottles that surrounded me on the living room floor, along with a half empty bottle of Remy, my night was pretty much self-explanatory. With the same clothes I had on the night before, I got up and tuck my gun in the small of my waist to open the door. She stormed past me with my daughter 'Winter' clinging on to her hand. When she saw me, she jumped in my arms, "Daddyyyy!"

I lift her in my arms and kissed her cheek while side eyeing Hennessy's ass. "Why you here so early Nessy? And what I tell you about just popping up to my crib?" I close and locked the door so I could sit down with Winter. "What time is it?" I asked.

She walked around my entire apartment like she was looking for something. "Ain't no bit..." my eyes focused on Winter and I knew her three year old ears sucked everything up so I chose a different word. "Ain't no females in here Nessy but if it was I'm sure you'd run her smooth the fuck away poppin' up like this... not cool ma, not cool at all."

Ignoring me, she went to the kitchen and grabbed a garbage bag from under the sink so she could pick all the bottles up from the floor and get my place back looking the way it was suppose to look without me even asking. Hennessy was beautiful but our time had run its course. We first started dating our freshman year of high school but ended up breaking up cause of my cheating and her off the wall ways and insecurities. I remember the first day I saw her... she was one of the flyy girls in school dripping in jewelry and designer shit. She was a short 5 feet even and fun sized but she was thick in all the right spots with chinky eyes, long natural lashes, and pretty light blemish free skin. Only thing I didn't like, were those raunchy ass lace front wigs she wore. She already had nice hair but being mixed with black and Hispanic, she always struggled with trying to fit in. Her name alone made her fit in, ghetto ass name sounding like she was going to work the pole. Her daddy Ramos was a bad alcoholic and when she was born, he named her after his favorite drink. I even offered to come up with some names and go pay for her to change that shit since she complained so much about it but she was too lazy to go through the process. "I'm sorry about what happen to Ronnie, but nigga I've been trying to call you all night long and you got yo damn phone powered off. You need to stop that shit, it could be an emergency."

I watched her with both her hands placed flat on the countertop of the kitchen and I knew she was about to start up. "Look, let me shower and make some runs. Imma be back to talk to you aiight... I promise."

She rolled her eyes. I kissed Winter again and played with her for another ten minutes as Hennessy stared in silence. I really couldn't read her but now wasn't the time and this was one of my other problems with her. Hennessy wanted everything to be about her but in the time of my grieving, she was still worried about her whether I showed how hurt I was or not. After showering, I walked out to Hennessy and Winter both knocked out on the couch with cartoons playing in front of them and walked out wearing a pair of basketball shorts, some J's, and a grey wife beater with the fitted cap draped over my dreads. I made sure I was strapped cause I was on a mission, that lil bitch Turquoise was gonna answer some questions today or on God she was gon' pay. As soon as my J's touched the bottom of the staircase in my building, I ran into RaRa dressed real simple in some ripped jeans and a tank top with a silk scarf around her head ready to make her way to my apartment. I had to stop her in her tracks, "I'll holla at you later RaRa... my baby mother and my daughter up there and I'm not in the mood for no fuck shit today."

"Are you fucking ya baby mother Gu? Keep that shit real cause I'm getting' real tired of this. I don't know nan other nigga that praise they baby mother more than you!" She raised her voice drawing attention to us knowing I didn't play that shit.

"Lower yo fuckin' voice Ra... I'm telling you, don't fuckin' disrespect me! That's the last thing you wanna do." I sneered.

"Say Ra! Shit, already heated round here, don't come over to this side with the ratchet shit ma! You too pretty for that shit. Yo Gu! If you drop her ass to that ground, I swear I won't say shit." My nigga Beans sat on the top of his tricked out Cutlass parked on the side of the street clocking the block. "Man going through enough, show some respect."

RaRa shift one leg to the other, "FUCK YOU BEANS! WASN'T SAYING THAT SHIT WHEN YOU WERE TRYNA GET THE PUSSY! FUCK OUTTA HERE!"

Beans chuckled again, "Awe RaRa please... nigga don't want that stank. Gone head on."

"You gonna let him talk to me that way?"

"You know Beans play all day. What the fuck is wrong with you broads. Guess you don't give a fuck about a nigga losing his cousin, more like a lil brother last night huh? A nigga can't even grieve in peace! I got my baby mother popping up on her bullshit and then here you come. Selfish ass females only worried about ya'll muthafuckin' self. Fuck yo feelings right now Ra!" I walked past her frustrated making my way to my Camaro. She was right behind me.

"Oh no, when the fuck you start talking to me like that Messiah?"

I turned around quick, "the fuck did you just call me?'

"You heard me! Messiah!" She sneered visibly angry.

Instead of putting hands on her ass, I dug in my pocket, "yo how much I gotta pay you to leave me alone for a few days RaRa? Foreal kidd, you wildin' you bein' super childish."

"Nigga don't play me like a trick!" She fumed. I turned my back on her ass to walk away again. I don't know what made her get bold and mush me in the back of the head but before I knew it, I had her ass hemmed up by the rim of her tank and pressed against the passenger side of my car.

"Let me explain something to you yo!" I grilled. "Don't you ever disrespect me and put hands on me again ya heard? Or else shit ain't gon' go like this... I promise you, and I don't give a fuck about yo punk ass brothers either." I let her go as she fell to the floor all dramatic and shit crying like I really fucked her up or something. Shaking my head, I crank the car and rolled the window down. "Go home Ra! That shit ain't cute!"

"Told yo ass!" Beans hopped off the car to help her, "ya'll females don't fucking listen. This world would be a much better place if ya'll simply fuckin' listened."

"GET THE FUCK OFF OF ME BEANS!" She snatched her arm away from him and used her hand to dust her jeans off.

"Well fuck you too then... shit, my bitch in the house nice, calm, and quiet like a girl should be. I ain't gotta help yo ass."

"Nigga please, yo quiet house mouse got more miles on that pussy than a Mack truck, fuck outta here." She mumbled and walked off giving me the eye.

A nigga cared for RaRa and all but the disrespectful shit was a 'no go' for me.

~~~~~~

I made my rounds for the day and as soon as I got back to 'Da Nolia' shit was live like nothing ever happened. I understood though cause death was so common around here the shit was starting to feel like normal routine.

"Sue!" I yelled walking into her apartment. She had the music going and was balled up on the couch with a pint size Tequila bottle in her hand.

"You know that damn Becka never made it here?" She slurred.

I walked over to her and grabbed the bottle, "yeah well this shit ain't gon' make it no better ma."

"Give me my goddamn bottle back! YOU LET THEM NIGGAS KILL MY BABY!"

That shit stab me in the heart, God knows I always tried to protect my cousin. "Man what?! You know what Sue, I'mma let that slide cause I can't even imagine how it feel to lose a child. What I do feel is what it's like to lose a brother, somebody close to me, and I ain't bout to let you make me feel more fucked up than I already feel... and where the fuck is Tuff?" I frowned referring to the only nigga that she ever let come around and play step daddy to Bari, Ronnie, and me. Tuff had been around for years and was a real smooth OG. He was a hood nigga like the rest of us and although he an older cat, he was aiight with me. Shit, it took a strong nigga to deal with Sue and her ways. "Nigga ain't never here and he's supposed to be here sometime Sue... damn, if you stop running the man away then maybe you can back up off me a lil bit."

Sue simply shrugged her shoulders... "out making money, where a man should be."

Bari walked from the back room shaking her head, "She's been doing this all night. I'm telling you Messiah, don't even say anything."

All of a sudden Sue started sobbing, "So ya'll gonna double team me today, huh? Goddamit ya'll didn't lose a baby, I did!"

"This is too much for me, I'm leaving this house." Bari grabbed her house key thinking I was about to let her ass out with that makeup shit on her face again. I sized her up and down... her lil outfit was aiight and age appropriate but that face had to go.

"Bari, I don't know what you get away with, with Sue, but I'm not wit' it. Go take that shit off yo face Bari, this gon' be the last time I tell you." And just so she didn't think this shit was a game, I sat there in the rocker right next to the door just so she didn't try to be on no slick shit and leave anyway.

Her face turned beet red from anger and embarrassment. "OH MY GOSH MESSIAH!" You think every dude will only want me for my face? If they gonna like me then why couldn't it be something besides that?" She fussed not backing down with her hands on her hips.

Bari was the only female I had some kind of patience with; and she only got the pass cause she was my sister. "Nah, I know exactly what all these lil niggas want and it damn sho ain't that fuckin' shit on yo face, but keep it up, keep makin' yo'self look older than your time and you gon' fuck around and get some shit you ain't lookin' for. Then I'ma end up in jail for killin' a fuck nigga who didn't know how to keep his dick to his self . They can do what they want to all these other lil fast ass girls... but not my fuckin' sister. GO TAKE THAT SHIT OFF!"

"STOP YELLING IN MY FACE MESSIAH!" She started to tear up; no matter how hard she tried to act, Bari was sensitive as hell.

I look from the rocker I was sitting in, and then back to her, which was at least five feet away. "How am I in yo face Bari? You way over there, and furthermore, that ain't even yo real face. Go take it off." I propped my hand under my chin and showed a expression of boredom while waiting. "Time is money and I got more to make, a funeral to plan and pay for, and business to handle."

The look of shock and rage covered her face but she knew not to say shit else. I didn't wanna be hard on Bari but I had to cause she was too damn gullible for me at times.

"Bout time somebody told her something." Sue slurred. "HE'S RIGHT BARI! STOP BEING FAST CAUSE MY HOUSE ONLY HAS ROOM FOR ONE WOMAN, AND THAT'S ME!"

"I'll be back later Sue, get up and get yo' self together." I kissed her cheek and walked out sitting on the staircase hoping to catch the chick Turquoise sooner or later. In the meantime, I called Becka... "Becka, although you may not care, can you at least act like it till Ronnie is in the ground? Go check on Sue, she may be under the impression that you may start to actually give a fuck." I left on her voicemail. After twenty more minutes of waiting on Turquoise ... it was still nothing, and a nigga was frustrated as I dialed Bambi's number. "What's the door number... of the chick Turquoise?"

She popped her lips loud and smacked while eating something. "It's 2b Gu."

"Thanks."

"But wait!"

"I said thanks Bam."

I hung up and made my way up the flight of stairs and through the pissy pew hallways smelling like a mixture of fried chicken grease and liquor. I tuned out the music blasting from behind the thin doors, the chicks sitting on the stoop braiding hair and gossiping, and the niggas rolling dice and talking shit. Everybody who was anybody wanted to try to stop me and talk or send their condolences, but I wasn't focused on none of that shit simply shooting everybody the head nod. My J's tapped every step until I was right in front of 2b not hesitating to knock.

As soon as the door swung open a thick brown skin chick greeted me... and when I say thick, I meant super thick. She was the real fucking deal but I wasn't here for shorty. Her face was pretty with plump cheeks and kinky eyes. Her thin lips were covered in some kind of gloss and her long hair was in a sloppy ponytail. Now on the other hand, she wore nothing besides a pair of black boy shorts with a wife beater with her stomach slightly hanging over. Before she even ask who I was, she made sure she pulled from her Newport and blew the smoke in my face first; it took everything to hold my composure and not drop her disrespectful ass cause first off, I wasn't a fan of females smoking cigarettes and I damn sho didn't play that whole blowing smoke in my face game; to me, that was the same as spitting in my face. From what I was able to see of the apartment, it could've been a little tidier but it was okay for the most part. "So you gonna tell my why you at my door or just stand there looking all handsome and shit cause that view is fine with me too." She smiled showing a bottom grill of gold teeth and much to my surprise, she sounded sexy as fuck, she had the most intoxicating voice I'd ever heard.

I licked my lips and gave her that 'she can get it look', that shit always worked. Anyway, my main focus was getting in the apartment. "My name is Greg." I lied, "but everybody call me 'G'... you new around here? I wanted to formally introduce myself."

A wide smile spread across her face and she was ready, I could tell, and I bet any amount of money that if I sat my hand in the seat of her panties my shit would probably come out looking like the Niagara Falls. The look on her face went from disapproval to welcoming with just a simple introduction and although shorty was bad... she definitely had a habit. I'd been around snorting muh'fuckas long enough to detect that shit without a test. Even if she wasn't consisted, I could still tell. I could've stayed out here and played this 'Mr. Nice Guy' shit all day but my name wasn't Doctor Phil and damn sho wasn't tryna get caught standing in front of this girl's door. Although I felt like I didn't have to answer to anybody, I still didn't feel like arguing with none of the chicks that felt like I owed them something all cause I fucked up and let them sample the dick.

Pretty girl extended her hand to mine and introduced herself, "Oh... that was nice of you... my name is Loraine but everybody calls me Rain." Her eyes averted to mine as her demeanor changed a little, she was nervous and I could tell. I'm not cocky but I realized I had that affect on women at a young age, especially when Sue's best friend Ms. Patrice, who was twice my age introduced me to manhood at the age of sixteen when she gave me some of the best pussy I ever had in my life. Till this day I'd always remember that. I was rocking my corn rolls and Ms. Patrice always kept my shit nice for me.... Kept my shit in the latest designs and all, especially the fishbone braids... them shits drove the girls' crazy. One day while sitting in her chair in the middle of the living room, I noticed she wore a short dress that showed a lot of thick thighs and toned legs. Shit barely covered her round ass; it kind of threw me for a loop a lil bit cause she never dressed like that before... well at least not around me. But anyway, she made it a point to keep brushing her breast and shit all up against me every time she went in to part my scalp, or she'd come stand right in between my legs when she needed to braid from a certain angle. Trying to ignore her advances, I just kept trying to think of shit to keep me distracted, like that upcoming Super-bowl game with the Miami Dolphins and New England Patriots; anything beside what I was feeling in my dick. I kept asking myself if I was tripping until she abruptly stopped and took my hand placing it on her bare pussy telling me, *"You a lil man now Gu... let me show you what some seasoned pussy feel like before you go sample them lil young girls."* She teased.

Now, on God, I thought the camera crew was about to come in and tell me I was being punk'd any minute, but when she took her dress off pulling it over her head all bets were off, and I knew that shit was real. Needless to say, Ms. Patrice fucked me so good... she had my young mind all fucked up thinking I was really in love with her and shit. After it happened once, it happened a few more times until she kept coming up with excuses as to why she couldn't braid my hair no more and since I wasn't letting nobody else touch my hair, I let my shit lock and dread up. I didn't know why she was tripping, but I soon found out when Sue told me Patrice was getting married. I was mad as fuck and I didn't give a fuck that she was in her 30's... she was MY BITCH! I wanted to kill her husband, real deal. Although I had Hennessy, I still didn't like the idea of Ms. Patrice getting married because Hennessy still hadn't given me any and when she did... I had to pretend we were actually losing our virginity to each other as planned. Shit was fucked up, I know, but it is what it is. Now I was standing here looking in Rain's face wondering if I should just see what shorty was on, or just pull out my burner and jack her ass up until Turquoise got here. It only took me a few seconds to decide that I couldn't play this shit cool cause if I did, they'd think I was a joke all around.

"So... can I come in? What you tryna do?" I held up a small bag of candy dangling it in her face. Just like I thought, her eyes lit up at the white powdered substance like she'd just hit the lotto or somethin'. Stepping to the side, she peak her head out in the hallway looking to the left and right with a wild look in her eyes like she was preparing to cross an busy intersection or something before gently grabbing my arm pulling me inside.

"Come on." She said excitedly.

See, this was the problem I had with females... too damn trusting. She could never be my girl though cause the way she just let me in her apartment with little persuasion... she'd get a nigga killed. She turned her back to lock the door and as soon as she turned back around... my gun was in her face.

Both her hands shot up in the air with confusion written all over her face. "Wha-Wha-What the fuck is you-you doing?" She staggered with her words knowing she'd just fucked up.

With a grimacing look, I told her straight up. "My cousin got killed the other night..."

"I don't know what happened!" She squealed with fear in her eyes.

I chuckled, pressing the butt of my gun into her temple as I slightly leaned down aligning my lips with her butterscotch smelling ear. "You talk to much ma... I wasn't implying you knew shit... but I know who does... where the fuck is yo sister?" I asked without letting up. Even with fear all over her face, the vibrations from my deep voice caused her to shutter as she licked her trembling lips.

"Look, fuck Turquoise... that's my sister and all but we don't rock like that... matter fact we got into it earlier today and I don't even know if she's coming back!"

Looking into her chestnut brown eyes, I was a pretty good judge of character and I could tell she wasn't lying, but I didn't give a fuck, she was gonna have to tell me something. "Where the fuck is she right now?"

"She's leaving school!" She finally let a tear fall with both her hands still in the air. "Look, I just wanted to have some fun with the candy... I wasn't expecting all of this!"

'What a waste of beauty'... I thought to myself. Bitch was fine on the outside and empty on the inside. "If you even mention this shit, I swear to God and everything I love you and everybody you love gon' pay."

Her eyes jumped back and forth and then back on mine, "I don't even know what you're talking about right now... mention what?"

I cracked a light smile, "that's a good girl."

Taking a long deep sigh, she close her eyes and spoke again, "please just go."

"You may wanna rethink yo move the next time instead of being so open to just letting strangers in ya crib lil mama... if the candy make you that weak than you should probably be looking into some help before the shit gets real bad." I informed her as I tucked the gun in the small of my waist... and just as cool as I walked in, I walked out leaving her standing there on stuck. Now where the fuck was this Turquoise bitch at?

Chapter 2

Turquoise (Qui) Edwards

"Okay class..." Professor Gonzalez started, "the homework is to take twelve photos with each of them applying 'the rule of thirds, contrast, and reframing'. Be sure to show the originals before the effects are applied... and please please please... no in house photos. This is visual communications people. I need to know that you're grasping every detail of what we are learning in here, so get out and see the world. Take some very detailed photos and be sure to share your links with me via Google drive (or) Google slides. Please have it turned in to me by next Tuesday at 6 p.m. This is a pass or fail grade... simple... and you'll get the extra credit points if I see you actually put thought and effort into your photos." He stopped and grimaced looking at his watch while I silently prayed he dismissed the class although it was 30 minutes too early. I hated these nightly college classes... I really did and personally, 10 p.m. was way too late to be getting out of class, but I didn't have a choice since I had to work my 'Little Caesars' job during the daytime. As if he was reading my mind, he said it, "Class dismissed! See you all next week... enjoy your weekend."

Within the quickness, I hurriedly slammed my books shut and tossed them inside of my bag. Grabbing my orange juice and cheese pastry that I'd been nibbling on... I rushed out the door dodging my classmates so I could run up out of here. I was almost a few feet away from the exit when I heard 'Hulk' yell to my back. "DON'T FORGET LECTURE HALL ON MONDAY 'EDWARDS' I'M PRETTY SURE MS. ANDERSON IS GONNA GIVE US A POP-UP-QUIZ IN OUR 'HISTORY OF FILM' CLASS ON WEDNESDAY!" He reminded me. Hulk was one of my over the top, rock looking white friends but he was helpful as shit, and he was a good study buddy. He had a nice tanned complexion and stood about 6'2 with a real defined muscular frame and black spiky hair that he always kept up to par. He always kept him self up and as ironic as it may have sounded... some days he look like he just came from a rock concert and some days he was designer down from head to toe even putting me up on some shit I never even knew about. I low key felt like he may have been crushing on me a little bit cause every class he'd walk in with my cheese pastry and Orange juice, and on birthdays and holidays he always made sure he brought me a gift.

With one hand in the air, I waved with my back turned, "Got it! I'll meet you at building 2 Monday morning... night Hulk!" I rushed out to my beat up Pontiac G6, which was sitting in the parking lot sticking out like a sore thumb. My poor baby was fucked up... literally, but I didn't give a shit because she got me from point A to point B as long as I kept a spare gallon of water and some coolant in the trunk cause it gave me heating problems every other day. I knew what the issue was, I needed a damn water pump but the problem was I couldn't afford one. I knew from one look at me nobody would expect me to be driving this kind of car but who gave a fuck? Yeah, I'm a pretty girl and all with smooth pecan brown skin, slim waist, thick thighs, nice ass, a few tattoos here and there... but my favorite was the sleeve of Cleopatra on my arm. I rocked my good hair in long faux locks that looked like my real hair, and I was aware that because of my big oval shaped eyes, button nose and full lips... I had a very exotic look about myself. People would often ask me where I was from explaining to me that I looked like I was from an island somewhere but I let them know off rip. I'm just a beautiful black girl born and raised right here in Miami-Dade County. No matter how I looked, or what their impression of me was... I was really just a simple girl and it didn't take much to impress me. At only nineteen years old, I was trying to do the best I could to get up out the hood and away from Rain's ass. I didn't know what was up with her and why her attitude toward me had been so bitchy and off for no reason. We were only two years apart but I loved my big sister, I cherished her cause that's how it should be, but for whatever odd reason, she acted like she hated me.

We grew up in a household with both of our parents and they were still together till this day but one thing they didn't play was leeching. Although, we were their only two kids they felt like when we turned of age it was time to go and since neither one of us had much money.... We ended up moving to subsidized housing in 'Da Nolia' where it was income restricted and went by income, which was cool for us. When we first started living there, I was the one without a job but now that I did have a little job, I'm on the list to get my own apartment and I told them I didn't care what building it was in, JUST DON'T PUT ME IN RAIN'S BUILDING! I requested that more so for me than her cause I knew she didn't wanna be forced to have to see me everyday, which hurt but it is what it is. This morning before class she started a big ass argument with me all because I cooked up the last package of noodles... shit, I bought them in the first place but just to avoid fucking her up, I left and went to class with tears in my eyes... I didn't get her at all. Every time I would ask my parents about it, they'd always tell me Rain loved me and always cherished and protected me when we were kids, but I didn't remember any of that. Matter-of-fact I didn't remember much of my childhood at all. I don't remember anything before the age of fourteen. When Rain first got her restricts at the age of sixteen we took our parents car for a joy ride and Rain allowed me to drive. BIG MISTAKE! WORSE DECISION EVER! I don't remember what happen, or how it happened but I do remember waking up from a six-month coma with no memory of the accident or my life before that. The only memory I had was pictures, and for the most part I was a happy child.

Determined not to let that shit affect me, I went on with my normal life but I did have to do home school and therapy for a year and even then, Rain was distant. I kept getting the feeling that maybe she wanted me to die, or like, she resented me for actually surviving the accident. Every time I'd call her out on it or mention it to my parents, they told me I was being ridiculous so I brushed it off... maybe I was. Now five years later, at the age of nineteen... Rain got better, but she still had her moments so I tried to stay out of her way. Like now, on nights like this I would've loved for her to just give me a ride to school since she was the one with a brand new whip, compliments of her deceased ex boyfriend Butta. It had only been a year since he had gotten killed in Overtown but Rain still grieved him like it was yesterday... he purchased her that brand new 2016 Nissan Maxima and left her with a little cash but she missed him, I could tell... hell I missed him too... Butta was my nigga, like the big brother I never had, and when I was going through my therapy, he always made sure I was good even when my own sister didn't.

Bringing me back to reality, I looked at the half empty gallon of water in my passenger seat and could've kicked myself for not checking to make sure it was full earlier. "FUCK!" I sighed rolling my eyes while grabbing it. After slamming my hood back down, I figured I could make it back to the hood and then stop at the corner store to get another gallon or some coolant if they had it. I turned the music up and made my way to the store with a pure attitude while reminding myself that it gets greater later. "How much?" I asked the dude behind the counter while shuffling my two dollars from my bag, cause I knew damn well it better not had been more than that. He gave me the price and I placed the money on the counter. I knew it was risky being out on 'death row' this time of night but I had to do what I had to do. The minute my sneakers hit the pavement again, I found myself caught up in the middle of a shoot out with bullets ringing from both sides of the streets. With big eyes, I couldn't move nor catch my breath as the fright took over me.

Blap!

From the side a bullet managed to find its way right through the gallon of water that dangled from my hand inside of my plastic grocery bag exploding. "Ahhhhh!" I finally hit the floor in the puddle of water. I felt like I was in the middle of a 'Wild Wild West' film.... I had never in my life been through no shit like this but I promised it was gonna be the last. With my head down on the pavement I mumbled over and over. "Oh God! Oh God!" I cried not even realizing that I was being snatched up from the back. "Noooooo! Let me Go!" I tried to fight and swing but whoever was grabbing me had a grip on me. Before I could even say shit else I was being slung into a car and shit was happening so fast, I didn't know what kind of car. In a flash we were speeding out of there. "Who the fuck are you!" I yelled with tears in my eyes. "Let me out and I promise I won't say shit about this!" I contemplated on trying to jump out but the nigga was driving way too fast with the look of anger in his eyes while he constantly peaked at the side and rearview mirror, I assume making sure we weren't followed. I didn't know what else to do beside try to fight so that's what I did, especially when he wouldn't stop the car... fuck it, if I was gonna die then so was he. Just like a spider monkey I reached over and jumped on his ass.

"The fuck is you doing!" he tried to steer with one hand and push me off with the other and still try to watch the road at the same time.

"Pull the fuck over! Pull over! Grrrrgggghhh!" I yelled to the top of my lungs, *'the fuck? Did I just growl?'*

Getting tired of my shit, he used one strong arm and knocked my ass back to the passenger seat causing me to hit my head on the glass, not hard enough to break it but the shit still hurt as I winced in pain and grabbed the side of my head. I was gonna kill this nigga... fucking monster! "Ouch!"

Finally pulling over, he was sweating and out of breath, as he pulled out his gun and grabbed me by my shirt dragging me out the car. "And you better not fucking fight this time." He growled with the gun pointed right at my head. The cool night breeze smacked my face and instantly dried up my tears. We were in an alley with nobody else in sight; just us and the headlights from the Camaro, and a nice Camaro at that. The alley was dark and I didn't like it but because of the lights, I could finally see his face and even in one of the most frightful nights of my life besides my accident... I could see this nigga was pure beauty. His dreads were perfect but it was his extremely thick eyebrows and long lashes surrounding those pretty brown eyes that intrigued me. The color of brown was so rare and distinctive that I didn't have an exact color for them. His nose was perfect and his lips were thick and full screaming 'pussy eaters' at me. I scanned his body frame and even that was perfect and ripped with a body full of tattoos. I was only 5'4 and he stood a few feet over me... if my estimate was right I'd say about 6'1 or 6'2. How could somebody so beautiful be such a monster? "Let me tell you something... Turquoise is it?"

How the fuck did he know my name? I thought to myself as my chested heaved up and down from my now ripped shirt exposing my wine colored lace bra that covered my size 34c cups. I'm sure my long faux locks were all over the place and I felt yucky with my now wet clothes on; my head was hurting and my knees were throbbing from hitting the floor. "How-how... do you know my name?"

"Just shut up." He growled not letting up off that gun in my face. "Cause if I wanted to kill you, I'd done it by now." He used his other hand to wipe the blood that trickled down his face from me scratching him. "The fuck were you doin' on death row this time of night? All the females around here know not to go on that street past a certain time... go figure, yo ass out there. The fuck you tryna do... get killed?"

I was confused beyond words right now, "you don't wanna kill me, you barely even know me, you've got a gun in my face but yet you're concerned about me being on death row?" I frowned.

Although he kept a straight demeanor, I could see in his eyes that he was tickled by my slick ass comment. "I got me a lil slick one I see..." he smirked a little. "Get back in the car." He demanded. I hesitated... "we still in a danger zone, now get back in the fuckin' car."

That's all he had to say to me and my ass was back in the car without a fight. I've never wanted to see my sister so bad in my life so I could tell her about all of this. Fuck our argument earlier. This time when I got in, I felt a little more relaxed but my guard was still up because I didn't know this dude at all. "Where you taking me?" I asked.

Silence.

"Helloooo?"

He flashed a disapproving look at me before turning his music up a little ignoring me.

My disobedient ass turned it back down, "Helloooo... Mr. Super saver, can you at least tell me where we going?"

He shook his head again and furrowed his brows, "I see you definitely ain't a lil baby that's gon' listen shorty.... But I'ma have to fix that." He looked from me to the radio, "and don't touch my shit again." He said in a strong, smooth, deep voice.

I sat back and closed my eyes, "Dear God, if I don't make it tonight... just know I repent right now for anything I haven't done in your favor. Please take care of my parents, my family, and even my crazy sister. Amen." When I opened my eyes, he was looking at me crazy. "What?"

"I told you I wasn't about to do shit to you and that's my word... now let me get where I'm goin' then I'll explain to you what I want with yo feisty ass... aiight? You should be thanking me for dodging bullets tryna save yo fuckin' life... how bout that?"

"My life?" I frowned. "I hadn't even thought about that... I hadn't even thought about what would've happened hadn't he snatched me up. I could be on death row dead right now. He gave me a disapproving look again. "You right... I'm sorry, and thank you." I mumbled deciding not to say anything else.

He didn't say shit either, just a simple head nod was all he gave before his phone was ringing and he picked up on the Bluetooth from the car. "Beans... everything A1?"

Another sexy ass voice blast from the other side, and I knew I'd heard that name before. "Gu... tell me you good my nigga... that shit was cra...."

"Wait hold up!" He disconnected the Bluetooth so he could talk on his phone without me hearing everything. *Gu?* I thought to myself... *so that's his name?* I kind of liked it. "yeah we good... I'ma lay low tonight and I'll be back that way tomorrow." I watched as he intensively listened to whatever it was the guy Beans was telling him before he hung up. When I looked up again, we were turning into 'The Hilton' and I recognized this side of town cause it was my old neighborhood... we weren't far from my parents house over here on the east side, which wasn't a suburb but it wasn't the hood either. He unlocked the car and stepped out as I sat with my arms frowned and my ass still plastered to the seat. When he realized I hadn't gotten out, he turned back around. "You comin'... and that's most definite... so get out."

I made sure I kept my attitude under control and played my every move correctly cause I didn't wanna get my damn head knocked into the glass again for not listening to his mean ass. I guess I took my time to get out so he came around and opened the door for me. Looking up into his eyes, he looked way calmer then before, which allowed me to relax a little and step out staring at the hotel. "I can't go in there."

He stopped at his trunk and popped it open rambling while looking for something. Even from a few feet away I could smell his 'Ferragamo Classic' cologne that tickled my nose. "Oh... you going." He said without looking at me.

I didn't know what it was about hotels, all I know was I just didn't like them at all. Didn't like being secluded in them and they made me feel unsafe. Every time it was time to go inside of one I felt sick to my stomach. For some odd reason, my voice trembled and I felt my water ducts filling my eyes with liquid. What the fuck is wrong with you Turquoise? Get your shit together. I tried to reason with myself but that shit didn't work... I just couldn't do it. Silently choking up on tears, I told him again. "Please don't make me go."

Hearing my voice caused him to look up in frustration. "Look, didn't I tell you I wasn't gon' do shit to you? I don't want yo pussy and I ain't gon rape you if that's what you thinking." He placed his hand on his chest for emphasis. "Do I look like a fuckin' rapist? A nigga like me look like I gotta take it?" he shook his head. "We can't go back to the hood tonight... and I really need to talk to you about some shit."

"What?" I asked curiously cause he caught me off guard with that shit.

"The night my cousin died... two nights ago."

Blinking uncontrollably I swallowed hard and thought back to what he was talking about... I was there on the stoop that night, however, I didn't know that was his cousin. Then it dawned on me... my stoop was so secluded, who could've even known I was there? It didn't matter cause I didn't have anything to tell. Taking a deep breath while thinking about my safety as well as his... I sighed while he studied me. "Look, I can't go in that hotel... and as crazy as it sounds I don't know why, I just can't and I'm begging you to please not make me."

"Aiight, look... I got another spot I can go to but this time I'm telling you... if you make me regret this shit. I'll kill yo lil ass and toss you in the Everglades to the alligators... you feel me?" He said in all seriousness and I could tell he meant it. "Here" He tossed me a sweater to put on over my ripped clothes. "Put this on and cover up before somebody thinks you my girl and I been beating on you and shit. Nigga ain't got time for no domestic bullshit."

I grabbed the sweater and gladly put it on... "thanks... and can you tell me your name please?"

He smirked, this was the second time he did that tonight and I loved it... I loved his dimpled cheeks even more. "You know my name." He replied.

I frowned.

"You heard my nigga Beans say my name when he called me on the Bluetooth in the car. I don't know why women play games like that. Ya'll some of the nosiest creatures that I know... and if you ain't pick up on shit else, I know you picked up on that."

I was busted and he knew it by my silence... he was too smooth for me.

"Un huh..." he said. "Come on ma, get back in the car."

I did as I was told and as soon as the door closed, my stomach started rumbling embarrassing the shit out of me. I tried to control it but it wouldn't stop.

Gu pulled off and looked at me in shock, "that flat ass belly doin' all that? When the last time you had a meal?" He lightened up a little.

The first thing I thought about was my parent's house and how close we were knowing that I could get a good meal there. The problem was battling about actually taking this stranger there, or if he'd even go. Fuck it, what was the worst that could happen. "Um, my parents live a couple of blocks from here and I know we're both guaranteed a good meal..."

"Nah..." he cut me off.

I swallowed hard trying not to go off... "trust me, it's harmless, we can eat and go. I'm not trying to pull a stunt and my peoples are real cool. I swear."

He lightly clenched his jaws, "you probably tryna get a nigga locked up for kidnapping or some shit."

"Well, you are kind of kidnapping me."

"At this point you've had plenty more opportunities to run shorty... but you still here."

I couldn't believe this boy, like how many times did he warn me he'd blow my head off? "Well, of course I didn't... I wanna live that's why."

He shook his head and I could tell I was getting under his skin now, "Goddamn man. Maybe I should've left yo ass where you was." He gripped the wheel with one hand and licked his lips. *Lawd I could've passed out watching that.* "Aiight, where we goin'? Tell me how to get there man... and I promise you bet not try no shit."

For the first time all day, a wide smile spread across my face. I know it was late but both my parents were like bats and I guarantee they were still up like it was 5 o'clock in the evening. I gave Gu directions on how to get there and in no time we were pulling up in the driveway of the one story row home. I could tell my mama had been in the yard cause her flowerbed was upgraded and the deep green grass was freshly cut. The huge mango tree was trimmed perfectly and it was beautiful. Both my parents drove Infinity Q50's only my daddy's was black and my mama's was a deep smoke gray, which they both were backed in side-by-side.

"Can't believe I agreed to this shit." Gu mumbled while rolling a joint in his lap. When he was finished he placed it in the console. "You can eat but don't even ask me cause the answer is 'no'. The only women I eat from is my ole girl, my aunt, and my baby mother."

I felt some way when he mentioned his baby mother and the fact that he mentioned her as one of the women he ate from. I don't know why, cause it wasn't like I knew this nigga like that but whatever. I knew my mama wasn't taking no for an answer and plus, I had country parents, both born and raised in Lithonia Georgia until they were eighteen and moved to Miami. "Okay, no problem." I shrugged and led the way to the door.

Before the door opened I heard the heavy footsteps knowing it was my daddy and as soon as the oak door swung open, I smelled his old spice before I even looked at his face. Jumping in his arms was my first reaction as I wrapped my arms around his broad neck hugging him, "Daddyyyy!" I placed small kisses all around his face forgetting all about Gu behind me. "I missed you so much old man." I joked finally giving him some breathing room.

"Shit, who old?" he laughed, "You better ask ya mama."

I playfully slapped his strong arm, "Ewwww TMI I didn't need to hear that." I muffled my laughter with blushed red cheeks; he was so embarrassing at times but that was my daddy. Handsome and playful and at 50 years old he looked damn good with not a trace of gray hair anywhere. He was a deep golden brown and wore his with long neatly twisted interlocked dreads all the way down his back. His mustache was always perfect and he kept his facial hairs cut low as well. My daddy stood about 6'2 like Gu and was cocky cause he stayed in the gym. I got my pretty color and good hair from him along with his full lips but everything else came from my mama. My daddy wore a simple wife beater and a pair of Polo pajama pants with crisp white socks on his feet. Finally acknowledging that I wasn't alone, he looked around me and his demeanor changed a little going from playful to protective. "You brought somebody with you I see." He extended is hand to Gu's to shake it, surprisingly Gu obliged and shook it back. "I'm Ricky, how are you young man?"

Gu nod his head, "I'm Gary... I'm good thanks for asking."

"And who exactly are you to Qui?" He asked.

Gu picked up quickly catching on that Qui was me... it was my nickname. He cleared his throat but remained serious. "We're friends."

"From?" My daddy asked.

"School!" I blurted thinking quickly.

My daddy nod his head in approval. "Well I tell you what..." He told Gu. "Qui has never brought no dudes around this house... had me worried thinking I was gonna be calling her Quinton instead of Qui for a minute. Come on in, hell must be about to freeze over." He laughed.

"Dad!" I pierced my lips in pure embarrassment thinking this wasn't a good idea all of a sudden. I didn't even know Gu like that and already my daddy was about to have him all in my business.

I could tell on Gu's facial expression that he was about to have fun with this since I drug him here and he really didn't want to be here. "Is that right?" He smiled showing his perfect teeth. "Well, I see we gon' have to change that... please... tell me more."

"How old are you son?" My daddy asked.

"Twenty-two." Gu told him.

"You smoke?"

"Daddy!" I blurted again. "Where's mama?" I push pass him walking in the house. "Ma! Come get yo husband! He's about to have my friend smoke those cigars with him that you don't like!"

From behind me, I heard Gu answer him. "Yeah, occasionally."

"Gotta respect a honest man.... Come on... Welcome to our home."

The door slammed and I didn't even bother to look back. By now I was all dried up and I managed to wrap my faux locks up on top of my head. Following the aroma of food I met my mama bent over in the kitchen looking for something in the pantry and when she found it, she stood up holding a container with strawberry icing in it. "Bingo." She turned around smiling wearing a floral colored housedress that showed her curves and flared at the bottom. I definitely was blessed with the body of a goddess cause I got it from my mama. Her long hair was part down the middle and pulled back into a sleek ponytail with her diamond-encrusted studs in her ear. She was a shade darker than my daddy, Rain, and I... she was actually on the dark side period but she didn't care cause the blacker the berry the sweater the juice. Her small round eyes were dressed up with some beautiful mink lashes and her lips wore a berry color on them. Just like my dad, she was fifty as well but they both could pass for 25. A lot of times when Rain, my mama, and I would be out together... people would think we were all sisters instead of my mother being my mother. "Hey Qui." She walked up kissing my cheek. "What'cha doing here baby girl? Why didn't you call me?" She busied herself icing the cake but before I could answer her, my daddy and Gu were rounding the corner.

"Benita, I want you to meet Qui's friend Gary..." He looked to Gu, "Gary this is my wife Benita."

Gu's eyes said it all. He was shocked not even believing that was my mama. Just like everyone else thought. He extended his hands and smiled.

"Nice to meet you Mrs. Benita."

Her eyes lit up, "Qui you must really like him." She glowed. "I've never seen you with a boy... hell, girl I was almost worried.... And he's cuteeeee."

"Ma!" I shook my head; this was too much.

"Same thing I said." My daddy agreed. "Minus the cute shit."

I caught Gu trying not to laugh and I wanted to shoot him the finger but since I didn't know if he still wanted to blow my head off if I tried some out of the way shit, I didn't.

My mama chuckled, "ya'll hungry?"

"I am..." I replied but now it was time for me to get Gu's ass back.

"I'm good." He replied. "But thanks for asking." He looked at his Cartier watch with me wondering how the hell could he even afford that. "Qui we don't have much longer."

I cleared my throat, "mama... Gary has this thing where he doesn't eat from other people. He only eats from certain women in his life so he doesn't want your food."

He looked like he wanted to kill me but at the same time, he shrug his shoulders.

"Trust me son... I use to think the same way. Can't trust these women, especially around spaghetti sauce." He pat Gu on the back, "but once you taste her cooking you'll see why I had to marry her ass and lock it down. Clink! Clink!" He laughed at his own joke.
I palmed my hand on my forehead, "oh gosh."

"That's right baby!" My mama agreed. "Ya'll sit down... Gary you gone eat one of the best meals you've ever had in yo life and I promise you that. You know that's a sign of disrespect to not eat my food... good way to hurt my feelings."

"Wouldn't wanna do that Mrs. Benita." He replied giving me another disapproving look.

I shrugged my shoulders; that's what his ass gets.

"Gary! You better eat that damn food! Put her in a bad mood and make me suffer tonight if you want to! I'll put'cha in the headlock next time you come back!" My daddy yelled from the back room back in front of his 55-inch flat screen.

My mama fixed big ass plates for us both with fried chicken breast, steak strips with grilled onions, collard greens, yams, honey cornbread, green fried tomatoes, a slice of strawberry cake on the side and a huge glass of kool-aide. "Now eat up." She told us before going to join my daddy. She didn't have to tell me twice. Ignoring the glares from Gu, I put my face down only focusing on my plate when I heard his stomach growl. "Eat up Gu." I whispered.

Looking at me sideways he shook his head again before picking up his fork to eat his food. "I'ma fuck you up." He told me, in which I ignored.

Needless to say, we fucked our entire plates up without leaving anything to the imagination and was as stuffed as two pigs after. I was all set to go until my daddy decided to pull out the old photo book embarrassing me showing Gu all of my old childhood pictures. He scanned a picture of me about ten years old sitting on a pony. "Where were you?" He asked me.

I shrugged my shoulders and took a seat on the arm of the couch.

"UN UN Qui! Get yo ass off my couch girl! Sit properly!" My mama snapped as she then pulled out another picture from me at some party at the age of 13.

"You looked innocent." Gu said under his breath being sarcastic. "Where was this?" He asked.

This was getting really annoying because the answer was gonna be the same. I DIDN'T FUCKING KNOW! "Ma... can we put these pictures back please!" I snapped... I didn't mean to but there's no way they could've imagined what I was feeling. It was like a hole in my heart feeling like I didn't even know myself.

Her and my dad both lowered their eyes while Gu sat there studying me like he wanted to snap on me for snapping on them.

"I'm sorry baby." My mama wiped a tear from her eyes, "I just keep hoping you'll remember if you actually see how happy you were."

"Remember what?" Gu furrowed his brows.

I stood up on both feet and was ready to go now. "WELL I DON'T! AND I WISH YA'LL LET THE SHIT GO!" I walked to the door and unlocked it ignoring the shocked expressions on both of their faces... all except for Gu.

"Yo, I'm sorry about Qui and her attitude... ya'll don't deserve that. Let me holla at her real quick." I heard him tell them both.

"She's been through a lot." My daddy replied. "let her go, she don't mean it."

Gu ignored them both because next thing I know, he was meeting me on the porch while I had my own lil break down trying desperately to control my feelings. "Yo, what the fuck is yo problem Qui?" He grilled me forcing me to look at him. He looked right through my tears and shook his head giving me that look again. "Before I even say shit else to you... you need to apologize."

Even with a heavy and broken heart, I understood where he was coming from. They didn't deserve that. With the tears running down my face, I went inside to apologize and when I came back out Gu went in... I assume to say his goodbyes. "Get in the car." He ordered and I did what I was told. The entire way to the west side of town was a quiet one until the ringing phone was answered through the Bluetooth again.

"Yeah?" He answered in a smooth calm voice.

"Messiah, I'm so sick of this shit." The girl said sounding exhausted.

"Hennessy... I never made it back cause I had shit to handle. I didn't ask you to pop up at my house in the first place." He told her.

She raised her voice, "you know what Messiah! Fuck you okay?" She said with her voice cracking.

He sighed, "Is Winter okay?"

"Yeah, she's okay!" She snapped. "Why can't you just realize how much I love you Messiah?" She started crying again. "You don't need those other girls... I'm all you need. Don't you remember how much we used to love each other?"

"What other girls Hennessy? You act like it's a slew of them." He replied agitated. I assumed this had to be the baby mother. "Look, you know I love you, but our time is up."

"Well why do you keep fucking me then?" She asked.

"I'll call you later Hennessy. I can't do this shit right now." He disconnected the call. I sat there minding my business in my own thoughts cause this had nothing to do with me. Without looking at me, this time it was he actually placing a call and another female answered but she sounded a little younger. "Bari... I need you to stay in tonight okay? Don't be in the hood hangin' out and shit until I get back tomorrow."

She sucked her teeth, "but Bambi invited me out tonight... to a party." She whined.

"Not tonight Bari... just do that for me."

"Damn..." She sucked her teeth again. "Why every time you in some trouble I gotta suffer?"

"Stop talkin' so much... a nigga ain't in no trouble but I'm not gon' explain... just listen to me. That's it."

"You owe me." She giggled with a change of attitude.

A little smile spread on his face, "I got you tomorrow ma." Now I'm sitting here wondering just who the fuck did he think he was? The pimp of the south with all these damn girls? It wasn't even my place to ask him but I did feel a little jealous. He hadn't given me any funny looks tonight... not one look to even make me feel like he may have been a tad bit attracted to me. When he hung up, we pulled up if front of a huge Mediterranean style home and parked the car. "Whose house is this?" I asked in awe.

He pulled two duffle bags from his trunk. I brought it for my sister so when she turns eighteen she has somewhere to go and get up out the hood."

"Oh my god" I gasped. "This is beautiful... does she know?"

"Nah... it's her birthday present but she still has two years before she gets this."

"And what you do with it in the meantime?" I asked.

"Yo... you got a lot of questions and I've already given you too much information." He walked to the front door with me following.

"Well, you have a lot of secrets... Messiah." I called him what the girl called him. "Why did you lie about yo name?"

He used the key to unlock the door without even looking back at me. Meanwhile, I was examining everything about him. From the guns on his waist to his strong calve muscles with just the right amount of hair on his legs. "Gary is my middle name, so technically I didn't... and let's not talk about secrets cause I see you may have some of yo own." He replied catching me off guard. I hated this shit, everybody wanted me to remember something about a life I knew nothing about... and now him to. This was too fucking much. I wasn't gonna cry this time... I swallowed the tears and followed him inside cause I had a feeling this was about to be a long night.

~~~~~~

The house was beautiful, like some shit from a magazine and I was surprised to see that he had the entire place fully furnished. It was a three bedroom, three bath with two floors and I was in love. Hell, I wished I was his little sister. "Did you furnish this whole place at once?" I asked in awe damn there scared to touch anything.

Gu was sitting on top of the island staring at me, not saying shit but just staring. "Here you go with the questions again... but nah not all at once. Been doing this for awhile." He admitted.

I wanted to ask another question but he was making me mad uncomfortable with the staring and shit. I didn't like it. "Come here." He demanded.

I frowned, "you know you're very demanding?"

"And do you know you talk way too much sometime? If I didn't actually like you a lil bit I would've killed you hours ago just for gettin' on my fuckin' nerves... now come here." He ordered with a lil more authority... shit had my pussy super wet. Had a bitch wanting to ask 'yes daddy' and shit. I slowly drug my aching body over to him realizing that I may had hit the pavement a little harder than I actually wanted to. On top of that, my head was starting to throb from where I hit it on the window in Gu's Camaro. I hopped on the island and sat just a few feet away from him but in a position where I could look him in the eye. I could still see the dried up blood from the scratch I caused on his face. I was surprised my nosey ass parents didn't ask about that... then again they were so intrigued with the fact that I actually brought a guy over there they probably didn't pay it any mind.

"I'm sorry about your face." I apologized as he ran his finger across the scratch.

"Don't even worry about it... it's gon' take more then a scratch to make me fold lil mama."

I furrowed my brows; I didn't like that shit.

He caught it, "what? You don't like lil mama?"

"I'm a grown ass woman, I'm nineteen goin' on twenty and I'm nobody's lil mama." I told him.

He wasn't moved at all, "well... you my lil mama now and I'ma call you what I want. That's my name for you aiight? So get use to it."

I wanted to fuss and debate... but I'm not gonna lie. I loved the fuck out of his bossy and demanding ways. Gu had the 'take no shit' attitude and as a man what he said was gonna go. "Tell me why you really wanted to be in my presence Gu, you were looking for me?"

"Sure was, and I found yo ass... right on death row bout to lose yo life and what good were you gonna be to me if I let you die?"

For some reason, that shit hurt. "So basically if it wasn't for you wanting to question me..." I found my eyes averting to look at anything besides him and those deep brown eyes. "You would've took a chance and let me die?"

"I mind my business..."

"So is that a yes?" I asked.

Swiping his hand across his face and taking a deep breath, he spoke again. "Look lil mama..."

"It's Qui..."

"Aiight... lil mama." He said disregarding me. "I wanna tell you a story of two cousins and how they became more like brothers so don't say nothin' aiight? Just listen."

"I got you..."

For the next thirty minutes he gave me his entire background on him and his cousin Ronnie and how close they were... he even told me how they became more so like brothers and everything. I swore I saw a tear in his eyes when he finished although he let none fall... even with his tough demeanor I was able to see he was grieving in the worst way but no matter what he said... I couldn't tell him anything he wanted to know.

"Listen Gu..." I took my soft manicured hand and placed it on top of his. He snatched his hand back, but I understood cause I would've done the same thing. "I'm very sorry about what happened to Ronnie and I hate that happened. I don't really know what to tell you but I really don't have much to tell. Yes, I was there... but I didn't see anything... well at least not much. Everything was so fast and in such a blur that I couldn't even tell you what the person looked like that did it. All I know is it was a dude... one person and not a whole bunch of people. Whoever it was, Ronnie was familiar with them because when the dude called his name... he turned around to greet him, only next thing I knew he was being shot up and I ran... didn't wanna take a chance on being caught or being an accessory to nothing at all."

He looked at me like he was studying me with his eyes squint, "So you didn't see his face?"

"No..." I told him swallowing a lump in my throat.

He nod his head and hopped off the counter, "tomorrow... I'll take you to yo car so you can go home."

Damn, I had done forgot all about my damn bucket. Hell, I even forgot about my job. "I'm suppose to open up early tomorrow at my job."

"Where you work?" He asked.

"Little Caesar's."

"I'm sleeping in so don't wake me up talking about we gotta go." He pulled a knot of money out of his pocket and peeled off two hundred dollar bills. "Here... you might as well call in as soon as you wake up."

I could tell he was still in his feelings so I didn't oblige... I took the money and stuffed it in my jeans. Next, he went to one of the duffle bags he brought in. "Here." He tossed me a pair of his fresh boxers and a wife beater. "Sorry, this all I got but you can put it on for tonight... you can shower in either bathroom upstairs and it's soap and towels in the closet."

"Thank you..." I mumbled walking up the stairs to find the huge bathroom with crystal shower doors and a princess sink, literally the bathroom was fit for a princess but the granite and crystal engraved in the sink had me in love. I slowly peeled every piece of clothing from my body and hopped in the steaming shower, which I enjoyed for the entire twenty minutes that I was in there. When I got out, I wrapped myself in a plush towel to dry off and then put on his boxers and wife beater. I had to roll the boxers twice in order for them to fit me snuggly but it was all-good. My tiny size six feet sunk down in the soft deep rug as soon as I stepped foot in the guest bedroom across the hall, but I jumped when I flicked the light on and saw Gu leaned up against the dresser waiting for me.

"Shit!" I grabbed my chest. "Gu! What the fuck?" I panicked. "What's wrong?" Although I had his stuff on, I still felt naked and exposed as my hard nipples poked out through the shirt; my round ass sitting perfectly in his boxers didn't help either. My smooth toned bowlegs were completely exposed and I just felt down right crazy, especially since I'd never been touched in that way by a man.

He pulled the first aide kit from off the dresser, which sat on the side of him. I didn't even see the kit at first. He pointed to my scraped up knees. "Let me put some peroxide and Neosporin on your knees for you... I know they all scraped up."

I slowly walk to the bed and hopped on top of it with my feet dangling from the floor. "Um..oh..okay."

He caught my hesitation, as he kneeled down in front of me. I sat there with my arms hiding my chest. "You ain't gotta do all that..."

"What?" I asked in all seriousness.

He chuckled, "Never mind."

I watched him as he took his time and poured peroxide on the gauze before dabbing my knees and then he used the tip of his finger to apply peroxide. Next he added some witch hazel pads and the a dry gauze on top with a small piece of tape to hold it. "In the morning, take this off and let yo knees breathe."

I had to admit, I felt much better. "Thanks... and maybe you should put some Neosporin on that scratch too."

He shook his head and stood up, "nah... I'll be aiight."

After he packed the kit back up and closed it back... I peeped him ignoring a call from some name called 'RaRa' with a look of exhaustion on his face. I figured it was probably another one of his girls who wanted to argue. This nigga had mad hoes... shit was crazy but I couldn't even blame them bitches cause Gu was a piece of work... God really put his hands on him when he created him. "I'ma be around aiight... so if you need me call me, other than that... goodnight."

"Night Gu." I smiled feeling much more comfortable around him than earlier.

I watched him walk out and turn the light off and as soon as he did... I pulled out my phone and called Rain. "What?" She answered rude as usual... I didn't even take it personal cause she answered everybody like that.

"Rain... it's me. I just wanted to apologize about the noodles earlier okay? I'll buy more tomorrow."

She giggled. "I don't care about no damn noodles I was trippin' over my own personal shit and I took it out on you. Where ya at anyway?"

I was glad she wasn't mad but I wasn't gonna tell her my business right now. "I'll explain tomorrow but I just wanted you to know I'm okay."

"Well I got some news too... I met this fine crazy ass nigga earlier but he came here looking for you."

My eyes almost popped out of my head, "What was his name?"

"He said Greg... and he was real mad too. I don't know what you did but you may wanna lay low for awhile."

"Fine nigga with dreads?" I asked.

"Yep... you know him?"

"Yeah... but I'll tell you about it later... and by the way. Greg isn't his real damn name." I chuckled just thinking about him and his fifty million alias names. "I'll see you in a few hours."

"Aiight Qui..." she replied before hanging up.

I pulled the covers back off of me and went to go and find Gu so I could ask him about showing up to my apartment but I couldn't find him anywhere so the last option was the master bedroom that held open double doors. Making my way across the huge room to the bathroom. I noticed the steam coming from the cracked door. *Shit! Shit! Shit! Don't even look Qui... stop being nosey and just turn around.* I tried talking to myself but the curiosity got the best of me and I peaked anyway nearly passing out when I saw the horse dangling in between his legs. He was leaned up against the wall of the huge walk in shower with his eyes closed just letting the water hit him. At first I thought he was maybe meditating or something until I saw him wipe the tears and then turn around ready to scrub down. I nearly bust my ass trying to get up out of there without getting caught but the shit fucked me up to see him in there hurt like that and it must've been hard trying to keep shit together in front of everybody. Once I made it back to the guest room, I decided to wait another 45 minutes before going to find him again, only this time he was downstairs knocked out on the couch with a wife beater and basketball shorts on. He was on his back with his feet crossed. Two guns sat on the table and another was tucked on his waist. I walked back upstairs to search the closet for a blanket and was glad I found not one but two. I used one to put over him and I used the other one to cover myself as I balled up on the loveseat before falling asleep.

~~~~~

"I'm sorry... I can't take you to yo car right now cause I got some shit to handle but when I get back I'll take you... matter fact just give me yo key cause you don't need to be nowhere over there." Gu told me when we arrived back at 'Da Nolia' a little after 2pm. I still had on his clothes and had my dirty clothes in a bag. I reached in my bag and passed him my car key.

"Thanks." I told him as we got out of his Camaro. For some reason more people were out than usual today. "What the hell going on?" I asked.

"Ion know... but come on lil mama." Was his response; we made our way to the building and when we got closer there was a line in front of somebody's door. Two beautiful women were throwing down in deep fryers that sat on top of tables having a fish fry of some sort with a full menu and prices hanging on the wall with clear tape.

"What the hell goin' on Sue?" Gu asked the woman with a frown on his face.

The 'Sue' lady ignored him but the other one answered. "We havin' a fish fry Gu... damn."

"For what Becka?" He asked.

"To bury my son, what it look like? Hell, we ain't have no insurance." She fixed another plate and passed it to a guy as she collected money.

Gu was so mad I think he wanted to kill somebody. "My cousin don't need no muh'fuckin' donations!" He fumed.

A pretty lil fly chick sat on the steps smirking, "They trifling as hell." She laughed.

"Yo Bambi, they scamming these people thinking they buying this shit for a good cause." He told her. "They know damn well I got insurance on everybody, Ronnie gon' be straight. Ion like this shit here." He told the girl. "And where the fuck is Bari?" He asked.

She looked like she was hiding something as she looked away from him and back to her phone shrugging her shoulders. "Shit, ion know... I'm not her keeper."

He looked back to me and looked regretful for some reason. "Look, I gotta go handle this shit for the funeral but if yo car is still there I'll bring it back."

"What you mean still there?" I tooted my nose in the air.

"I mean... you did leave the shit on death row, them niggas probably stripped the whole car and sold it for parts... who knows."

That made my heart drop, that was my only means of transportation and I loved that car. Speaking of cars... I looked just in time to see Rain's car being hooked up by a tow truck with Butta's mama right there giving orders. I knew that shit was gonna happen sooner or later since the car was in Butta's name and his mama couldn't stand Rain. "Shit." I mumbled under my breath... I gotta go." I told him taking off, not that he was paying me much attention anyway.

"Rain!" I burst through the door. "Rain! Butta's mama is out here stealing your car!"

I knew that would get her to answer... she came rushing from the back looking like she'd just woken up with a bat in her hand. "Oh no the fuck this bitch didn't! I'll beat the whole fucking car to the ground before I let her just take my shit!" She rushed out and I rushed out behind her hoping that Gu was long gone cause shit was about to get ugly and the last thing I wanted to do was for him to see me acting all ratchet. But Rain was my sister so I had her back... fuck it.

Chapter 3

Belcalis (Bari) Carter

"Age ain't nothin' but a number, throwing down ain't nothing but a thang, this something I have for you... it'll never change."

The flickering from his tongue is what drove me crazy, it was the way he caressed my body, the way he felt me up and the way he made passionate love to me is what made me love him. He was my-everything, my sugar daddy, my rock, and my best friend. When I turned eighteen I was gonna marry him and I couldn't wait to run off with him. "Ouuuuu." My body shivered as he filled me up with my young legs spread wide open inviting him without a fight. I placed both of my hands on his ass and pulled his strong body close to me. "I love you, I love you, I love you." I whispered in his ear as he stroked me nice and slow just how I liked it.

Nuzzling his beard in my neck, he told me... "I love you too Belcalis... I love you too. Now hush now... just enjoy cause we don't have that much time." He groaned with his eyes closed enjoying every part of me. He lift him self from my body and held my legs back over my head, which didn't hurt me cause I was flexible as hell. I watched him lightly let spit fall from his mouth and fall on my swollen clitoris. "Do that thing I like baby." He continued to pump.

I took my two fingertips and placed them on my nub and pressed down in a rotating motion. "Sssss oh my God." I bucked my hips and pumped my pussy against him feeling my body heating up.

"Umm hmmm." He was pleased. "Now do that other thing I like... you know how to make me cum."

I used my free hand and grabbed my breast as I used my tongue to flicker it back and forth over my hard nipple while looking him in his eyes. Everything I knew about sex, he taught me and anything else I wanted to know about, he tried his best. Ever since he took my virginity two years ago... it had been on and popping. All it took for me was to do all the freaky shit that he liked and he was pulling out of me rupturing all over my stomach. "Why you do that?" I asked looking at him crazy. He never use to do that shit before. With sweat dripping from his forehead, he took the rag he had on the side of me and wiped me down before laying next to me cuddling me in his arms. "What's wrong babe?" I asked him.

"Look Bari, I love you and all but I can't risk you getting pregnant again. Luckily you were able to get that abortion through Bambi's connections but we may not be so lucky next time." He told me reminding me of that God-awful experience less than a month ago. I promised myself I wouldn't think about it again after it happened but it was super hard not to. How could I shake the feeling of laying on the cold table all by myself, or the pain I was in after the fact. Hell, I was lucky that Sue and Messiah even went for the whole bad period cramp theory. I was in so much pain that I had poor Messiah ripping and running to get me all kinds of meds and pain pills; I think he wanted to cry for me he felt so bad. My own nigga wasn't even there for me but yet and still, here I was in this crappy hotel room giving him my body again because I loved him.

"I understand." I told him. "I can't wait till I get of age so I don't have to hide this shit anymore. Like, I just wanna be exclusive with you... I love you." My lips trembled. I was so in love with him that most days I thought I would be sick when I didn't hear from him. I knew he was busy running his mechanic shops and stuff but I still wished he made time for me. I could understand why he didn't wanna be caught with me since he was twice my age but still... if it were up to me, I didn't give a fuck.

"In due time..." he replied. "In due time... now get some sleep." He told me before dozing off leaving me in deep thought. It was crazy how Messiah thought I was so innocent and he tried to keep me away from all the young boys. It's the old guys he should've been worried about cause that's what I liked. I kept telling him over and over to get off of my back but he just wouldn't listen. Everybody thought that Bambi was the fast one but in reality, she was quite calm and it was me who couldn't stop getting my pussy licked on and beat up. Bambi had actually only had one sex partner, which was Ronnie and they stopped fucking a little bit before he died cause neither one of them knew how to stop playing games. When it came to me though, she was always telling me to slow my ass down, especially after I had that abortion. Most of the time when I'd lie and tell Messiah I was invited somewhere with Bambi or that I was with her somewhere, it was a lie and it was mostly my alibi to get right where I was now. Looking into my bae's smooth mocha face; my heart skipped a beat and I was in love all over again. Right here in his arms is where I'd stay if I could.

Crazy even thinking about it though; this shit wasn't new to me and this went back as far as I could remember. When I was younger and Sue was in the streets hustling for us... Messiah was always with Ronnie and me... I didn't have anybody besides Bambi. It started off with me taking simple shit from older guys. Shit like candy, a dollar here and there, a ride home from the bus stop every now and then and etc. It got to the point that I was feeling like I actually needed someone older to complete me. It was so bad till the point that younger boys my age was a big turn off cause they couldn't do shit for me. Another reason why I wore makeup... I wore the shit cause I didn't wanna look like a little ass girl. It was clear that I was very developed for my age... but what can I say? I ate all my veggies? Real shit, I did. Bambi was the only person who knew about my extra curricular activities and that's the only person who needed to know. I didn't even tell Sue when I started my period at the age of twelve... and I damn sho didn't tell her when I started fucking although I'd been masturbating longer than that. A part of me kind of resented her because I felt like as her child and only daughter, she should've paid more attention to me. The more she acted as if she didn't care... the more lit I got and stayed finding more shit to do. School days went by and I was making straight A's, but I was also bored with life... period! And the only person who gave me the pleasure that I needed was the love of my life.

~~~~~

I ended up dozing off after awhile and when I woke up my man was long gone and just like always, he left money for me to do whatever I pleased with along with a little 'I love you' note that made me smile. I forced my naked body out of the bed and made sure to take a quick shower before redressing and ordering me a 'Lyft' to take me back to 'Da No' before Messiah or Sue started to notice I'd been gone. "Drop me off right here." I told the driver refusing to let him let me out near my building, so instead I got dropped off around the corner on death row where I had no fucking business at but since it was still daylight out I should've been okay. My crisp Nike Airmax hit the pavement as the disrespectful ass heat plummeted my face. My tight fit tank exposed my bare shoulders and showed my belly ring, and my skin glistened from little perspirations of sweat building up on my body. I was surprised how dead it was out here today and if Messiah knew I was over here I know he'd kick my ass. The only signs of any action was from the lil rugged niggas who were too busy to pay me any attention because they were stealing parts off of some beat down ass Pontiac G6 that looked like it was abandoned on the side of the road. Shaking my head, I continued on my way ready to hit the corner and get home.

As soon as I passed the store this lil dude named Dro who went to school with me was walking out the store with a gallon of milk to his mouth drinking it like it was a cup of milk. I couldn't stand Dro cause he was a fucking bully and was always beating somebody up... he was a grade higher than me since I was a junior and he is a senior, but still... he got on my damn nerves. I tried to look straight ahead and ignore him like I didn't even see his ass. "Yo Bacardi!" He walked across the street meeting up with me just as I got to the light to cross... fuck!

I turned around with a frown on my face, "It's Bari!"

As he got closer, I tried to walk faster causing him to chuckle. "I know yo fuckn' name! Why the fuck yo lil scary ass walking so fast?!" He barked still walking behind me. I'm not gonna lie, I wasn't a punk by a long shot but I was scared of Dro's crazy ass. He was cute and all, but just crazy and that light skin and grey eyes just wasn't enough to make me want to even get to know him... not even a little bit. "Slow yo ass down yo!"

I snapped without looking back, "I don't know who the fuck you talking to! You can't even say my fucking name right!"

That made him laugh even harder, "You know all you pretty bitches is the dumbest ones?"

That made me turn around and stop in my tracks to look him dead in the face, "now come on Dro... why you gotta disrespect me? It ain't even worth all that." I let his ass know. Just then a boy who I actually did get along with came across the street from one of the abandoned apartment buildings wearing his pretty black hair cut low with waves and a fresh tape. He was the color of caramel and he also had a fine ass face with juicy ass pink lips. He wore gold teeth in his mouth and was perfectly built. It never failed that every time I saw him he was designer down from Gucci, to Saint Laurent, to

Ferragamo... you name it, he had it and I didn't know how. He was also older than me, and a senior at our high school as well, but he was well respected.

"Yo Dro!" He walked toward us with a frown on his face as he tucked his chain in his shirt. "Leave that girl alone man... the fuck is wrong wit'chu?"

My heart started racing as I wondered why Pete was taking up for me and shit cause it wasn't like I was his girl. Dro looked to Pete not pleased at all that he was getting in his business as he frowned and sucked his teeth. "Nigga wasn't nobody gon' do nothing to this stuck up ass winch."

Me and my smart mouth just couldn't hold back as I snapped my head back like I was being punched in the face. "Your bald head ass mami is a winch." I told his trifling ass. Although I was talking shit, I was prepared to take off and run if I had to but to my surprise he started laughing like he was crazy and continued talking to Pete.

"Like I said, ain't nobody fuckin' with this girl."

Pete simply shook his head, "yo it don't matter, you gotta chill and leave these girls alone man. That's probably why you don't get no pussy... you gotta grow the fuck up yo."

I could tell Dro was embarrassed that Pete had put him on the spot although he didn't want me to know. I watched as he placed his milk gallon on the ground and balled his face up. "You wanna fight over this trifling ass bitch? This lil hoe ain't shit anyway... bitch round here fuckin' a grown ass nigga and think nobody don't know about it."

My entire fucking heart dropped! Nobody knew my fucking business so how did he even come up with some shit like that? Before I could even defend myself... Pete was all over him with one swift punch that took his ass to the ground and made him eat the floor. "Nigga didn't I just tell you stop disrespecting this fucking girl!" Pete fumed.

"Ahh! Aiight man! Aiight! Get yo fuckin' knees up outta my neck!" Dro begged.

Pete went harder, "nigga I'm bout to make a concrete sandwich outta yo fuckin' face! Apologize!" He dug his knee harder into his neck.

Dro's face wore agonizing pain as he finally gave in, "Okay! Okay! I'm sorry aiight Bari? Nigga apologize!"

"Apology not accepted." I rolled my eyes, "fuck you... and thanks Pete." I stomped off.

After the scuffle, Pete pulled out his gun making Dro get the fuck outta dodge and then caught up to me and started walking along side of me. "Why you on this block?"

I shrugged, "cause I didn't wanna get dropped off in front of my building..."

"This shit dangerous." He warned.

I nod my head, "yeah I know and it won't happen again."

"Yeah, I bet if yo big brother found out you was over here getting' disrespected it would've been on and poppin'."

I stopped and gave him a serious look, "yeah well he won't find out... right?"

Pete laughed it off, "I mind my business."

I couldn't do shit but laugh as we started walking again, "You mind yo business huh?" I smirked with an eyebrow raised.

"What that mean?" He asked.

"Dro... that was you minding yo business?"

He threw both his hands in the air and laughed again, "yo that was different, and don't act like you don't know a nigga been checkin' for you since freshman year Bari... you just be on the bullshit."

I bit on my bottom lip thinking about what he said cause it was true... "Look, you have never seen me talk to no boys my age like that, especially at school so don't take it personal Pete."

"Why is that?"

"The truth?" I asked. See that was the thing, people wanted the truth but it didn't mean they could handle it.

He frowned as we got closer to my building. "Nah, I want a lie... the fuck? Of course I want the truth."

"Well, can't no nigga my age or in my school do shit for me, that's why."

By now we were in front of my building and I was mad our walk ended so quickly cause I was enjoying talking to him. He was listening to me but at the same time, he was distracted by a group of chicks from our school walking into the basketball court wearing tight ass jeans and booty shorts. He turned back to me quickly. "Look, I hear you and all but that ain't the way to think."

I crossed my arms in front of my chest, "is that right?"

"Yep." He smiled. And oh my God his smile was gorgeous. "But look, I'll see you around aiight? You be easy." He told me back peddling so he can still talk to me.

"Yep! I bet!" I waved.

He chuckled as the sunlight reflected from off his gold teeth, "aww don't be like that Bacardi!" He said mocking Dro trying to be funny.

"Don't play with me!" I said laughing at his backside since he was now headed inside of the basketball courts.

Turning around, I took a deep breath to head upstairs but before I could get to my door, Bambi was opening her door, which was a few doors down from mine. She wore a simple pink fleece with some tory Burch slides on her feet, and she looked high as a kite. "Girlllll!" She gently snatched my arm up causing me to stumble into her apartment.

"What's wrong with you?" I asked frowning when I got inside not even appreciating her grabbing up on me like that. "What happened?"

"Gu was looking for you." She informed me sitting on the couch rolling another joint. Not that she was worried about getting caught, hell her mama was never home.

"Okay, and what did you tell him?"

She looked at me with furrowed brows and I admired her beauty, my best friend was too pretty. "Shit, I didn't tell him nothing, I told him I didn't know where you were cause I didn't... shit, bitch you slippin' cause you normally tell me the alibi so we can be on the same page."

I sighed and flopped on the couch, "man I know but it's just this nigga of mine be having me gone sometime... like my mind really be gone."

"You need to slow down Bari." She told me in a different tone. "For one, you don't wanna end up pregnant again and for two... you just wrong... period."

This was the shit that was gonna piss me off, and get my fucking blood to boiling cause people was always tryna tell me what the fuck to do. I stood up not wanting to even have this conversation with her. "Yeah, okay Bam... whatever." I rolled my eyes just as my iPhone started ringing. My eyes lit up when I saw my man calling. "Hello?"

"Who the fuck was the lil nigga you let walk you home?" He asked in a calm voice since he never raised his voice.

"That was a friend from school." I told him honestly.

Bambi took one look at me and already knew what time it was. She stood up shaking her head, "I don't know when you gon' learn." She mumbled walking into the kitchen.

"You givin' that lil nigga some of my pussy?" He asked almost in a growling whisper that caused me to cringe.

"No baby, of course not.... I swear." I tried to convince him.

"Belcalis... if you ever do some shit like that... I'ma kill you... you understand don't you?"

I swallowed hard thinking about the last time he thought I was doing something and slapped the shit outta me... luckily Messiah was out of town so he didn't see my face and I used my makeup to cover his handprint from my face when I was around Sue. "I promise nothing is going on baby."

"I don't wanna catch you talking to no more of them lil niggas you understand? I'm all you need... they can't do shit for you."

I gave a simple reply feeling defeated and I hadn't even done shit, "okay."

He didn't even tell me he loved me or nothing, he just hung up which let me know he was mad, and furthermore I didn't even know how the hell he was able to keep tabs on me like that.

"So what happened?" Bambi asked leaning up against the wall munching on some hot Cheetos.

"Nothing." I told her unlocking the door and stepping out into the hall with my heart throbbing. "I'ma check you later."

"Um hmm." She rolled her eyes and sighed. "Just know I'll fuck that nigga up if he puts his hands on you again." She told me causing a slight smile to escape from my lips.

I walk to her and pulled her into a hug as we embraced one another. "I love you bestfrannnn." I sung.

"Cause my bestfran finna, she finna, ohhhh go bestfran that's my bestfran, that's my bestfran.... I love youuuu." She playfully sung back.

If she only knew how I was really feeling inside... I loved Bambi with everything in me and she was the only real friend I had... that's why I felt bad for not telling her that I found out I was pregnant... again! And just that fast. My heart was crying out for help and I knew I was fucked up inside. I was trying to fill a void but I didn't know what exactly it was. Before I knew it tears were in my eyes.

"Awww what's wrong Pooh?" Bambi asked concerned.

I quickly wiped them away not wanting to tell her shit yet, "Nothing... but I think I may have a friend for you." I thought about Pete.

"He got a beard? Or some kind of facial hairs?" She asked cause now a day's niggas were freshmen with full grown facial hairs.

"No." I giggled.

She pushed me back out the door shaking her head, "Un un... nope! Cause if he don't got a beard I can't even take him serious."

I fell out laughing, "You wrong Bambi!"

She looked at me shocked with her eyes wide, "What bitch? Ain't you heard that beard game matters? He gotta be 'GANG GANG' in this bitch or I don't want him. Bye." She slammed the door in my face brightening up my mood.

Still laughing at Bambi... I made my way down to my door and noticed the chick Turquoise on her stoop giving me a weird look, but when I looked at her she tried to act like she wasn't looking. I didn't know what was up with that but I ignored it and walked inside straight to my room throwing myself over the bed with tears welled up in my eyes. I felt bad... real bad about a lot of shit and I missed Ronnie too. I wish I could've just heard his voice or talk to him one last time but instead I was about to get ready to bury him. Shit sucked.

Chapter 4

Rayliris (RaRa) Almanzar

"Like a baseball field, wanna hit a home run, me and you get together babe, and raise a little one. Half on a babyyyyy, all I need is your body next to me."

"Open the door RaRa! It don't take that long to pee on no damn stick! Hoe I wanna see!"

"Go away! Let me take it all in for a minute!" I yelled from the other side sitting on the toilet all boastful reading the results of my pregnancy test. I had been feeling a little down and lazy for the last couple of weeks and when I missed my period it was all the confirmation that I needed. It was official.... I was finally gonna be a mommy and Gu was gonna be a daddy again. I knew from the first time I laid eyes on Gu that he was gonna be my baby daddy but the nigga was so careful with his protection, I seriously doubted it would ever happen, that's why I had to poke a few holes in through the condom wrapper when he went to use the bathroom one drunk night. I knew my ovulation down to the 'T' and all I needed was the opportunity. I mean, I knew if I'd told him straight up that I wanted a baby from him he would've never went for it, especially since he told me over and over next child he had would be from his 'wife' if he ever got married... but 'oh well' it happened and I wasn't killing my baby, period.

He'd been acting funny for the past couple of days and after my girl Tricia told me that she saw him flaunting around with some new bitch from 'Da Nolia' I wasn't having that shit and wished even more that the test came back positive when I got ready to take it. Besides, you had to be careful with these niggas and whom you chose to have a baby from. Gu was the perfect package, he wasn't no broke ass nigga, he was fine as fuck, and on top of that I saw how good of a father he was to his daughter 'Winter' so I knew he'd be a good dad to our baby too. Now Hennessy wouldn't be the only baby mama he'd be praising. Since he loved his other baby mama so much, he'd praise me too.

"RaRa! Come on damn!" Tricia refused to let up off my bathroom door. Rolling my eyes, I wrapped the tissue around my hand and then wiped myself before flushing and getting up. When I opened the door, she was standing there waiting for me. "Bout time bitch... what it say?" She asked snatching it from me. Her eyes grew wide and a huge smile spread across her face. "Bitchhhh you're pregnant!" She jumped up and down like it was her test or something.

I snatched it back and tossed it in the garbage like it was nothing. "Yep, and you gonna be the godmama." I informed her while pouring me a glass of sweet kool-aide. Tricia was my best bitch and had been since we were rocking in the sand on the playground back in the day. It was simple, no bitches were allowed to fuck with her and vice versa or you had to be prepared to deal with the both of us. Right now I was living with her and her nigga 'Swain' since me and my auntie kept getting into it and now that I was pregnant, I knew I was gonna have to get a job and grab my own lil spot. It was a good thing that Tricia lived a few blocks away from 'Da Nolia' and not directly in the place cause I was damn sho bout to be hiding out from Gu's ass until it was clear to tell the world about our precious baby. By the time he found out I'd be way past the abortion stage as long as people minded their fucking business... everything would be okay. After I drank down my cup of juice, I turned back to Tricia and examined her. Tricia wasn't the prettiest girl but she had a big heart. While she was light skinned, she had a bad case of acne and her nose was a little on the protruding side. She did however have some long beautiful and thick hair that she wore in a long wrap and her body was decent. She was as thick as the rapper 'Trina' and was all that in the body area.

"I'm not telling Gu!" I blurted.

She frowned, as I knew she would since she was sometime on her holier than thou shit. "Why the fuck not?"

"Because, if I tell him he's gonna make me have an abortion and I'll kill that nigga first. I'm having my baby and that's just that."

"But I don't understand why he would be acting such a way RaRa... like why even take the chance of not using protection and then get mad when somebody pops up pregnant?" She shrugged popping a cracker in her mouth, "the shit makes no sense to me at all."

I hadn't told Tricia shit about what I'd done cause I knew she would have a whole lot to say, so instead of addressing what she'd just said... I started fidgeting. I grabbed a plastic plate to heat up a leftover slice of pizza and tried to busy myself without looking at her. Sensing my hesitation, she walked over and slammed the microwave door as soon as I opened it. "RaRa! What the fuck did you do bitch? I'm not stupid and I've known you wayyyy too long!"

Sucking my teeth I looked at her with scolding eyes. Since we were kids Tricia always thought she was my mother since she was a year older than me and since she was always the logical one she was always trying to preach to me cause we were surely like day and night. A lot of people didn't even understand how we were even friends. "Look, it don't matter what I did... I wanted a baby and I wanted a baby from Gu, so I did what the fuck I had to do."

"What did you do?" Swain asked walking in the kitchen right in the middle of our standoff. We were so engrossed in our conversation that we didn't even hear him come in. Usually when he walked in he was making a bunch of noise. Today he was chilling. Standing at an even 5'11 and a dark mocha color, he rocked long dreads and a thin cut beard. Swain had a nice toned body and was always dressed in fly shit. While he was also considered 'that nigga' he was a legitimate nigga and went to work at a construction site everyday making good money. Hell, Tricia didn't work either but he worked enough to take care of them both while she went to school to become a paralegal. They were on some real Romeo and Juliet type shit. They'd been together since middle school. Technically Swain liked me first but since I wouldn't give him no play, I guess he chose the next best thing, which was Tricia. Till this day I knew he still had a thing for me, especially when I caught him looking at me from time to time but I'd never hurt my friend like that; and I wasn't interested in Swain anyway. He kissed Tricia on the cheek, "damn bae, why you lookin' at Ra like you wanna kill her ass?"

"I'm about to smack the fuck outta this dumb bitch." She hissed. "Yo, you embarrassing as fuck RaRa, you be on the dumb shit."

I knew she was mad but she better had watched her fucking mouth, "I'mma charge that shit to the game and act like you ain't say that cause if you put those fucking hands on me bitch we gone go blow for blow just like back in that day." I reminded her ass; Tricia and I had plenty of fights back in the day and always made up right after. That was how we released our anger toward each other. We'd have a good old fashioned fight and then act like it didn't happen.

Swain looked confused, "hold on now... ya'll trippin forreal. Why you wanna slap her bae?" He smirked. "Ya'll crazy."

Instead of answering the bitch slapped me forreal.

Blap!

"You dumb bitch!" She blurted. "I swear I got some dumb ass friends but you put the icing on the cake!" She tried to lunge at me again like a bull with her cheeks red and full.

She didn't have another time to hit me, and just that quickly, I forgot all about my pregnancy as I tried to reach around Swain and get to her. He used all of his strength to keep us apart while backing a hyped up Tricia into the corner.

"You lucky yo nigga here Tricia, or I promise you would've got these hands! And bitch if I'm dumb then you my best muthafuckin' teacher! Remember that!"

"Fuck you Ra!" She spat still trying to get away from Swain. "I'm sick of you embarrassing me with yo dumb shit!"

"Fuck you too Tricia! It's my pussy NOT YOURS! YOU ACTIN' LIKE YOU THE ONE WANTED A BABY FROM THAT NIGGA!" I barked noticing a change in her demeanor as she calmed down and her eyes glistened.

Swain looked at me with regretful eyes and then anger. "Why you gotta go there Ra?"

"FUCK HER!" Tricia was now wiping her tears leaving me mad confused. Like, what in the entire fuck was she even crying for? I'm the one that got slapped, and my face stung like a motherfucker.

"You pregnant Ra? From who?" Swain frowned but I saw under that shit... he was pissed the fuck off and I wondered why Tricia never caught the lil looks he gave me.

"I am, and I'm keeping it and that's all that matters."

"But from who?" He asked again.

"Yeah, tell him from who and how you even got pregnant Ra..." Tricia taunted.

I grilled her with my eyes; "yo what is it to you Tricia? As long as you the god mama that's all that matters... damn, I'll say it again, you act like you wish it was you or something."

"WOULD YOU STOP SAYIN' THAT BULLSHIT!" Swain snapped shocking me. What the fuck was his problem?

"You don't have to defend me bae... to hell with Ra and her slick ass comments." Then she looked me dead in the eyes and told me some shit that hurt my heart for her. "I can't even have kids RaRa... so you right, no matter how it happened... congrats bitch... kudos." She pushed pass Swain and stormed in the room.

"Tricia! I-I...." I tried to apologize but before it could even get out of my mouth she slammed the door in our face.

Swain looked at me like he wanted to hurt me. "You happy now?"

I plopped down on the couch placing my hands over my face, I felt like shit. "No I'm not happy Swain, what kind of question is that? Like why wouldn't she tell me that?"

"I tried to tell yo ass to shut the fuck up Ra... damn... you just don't listen fo' shit."

"I said I'm sorry Swain...."

"Yeah... well tell my girl that cause she the one that needs to hear it."

I took a deep sigh, "I know."

"Who you pregnant from Ra?" He asked standing directly over me. I felt his presence but I just didn't wanna look up.

"I can't tell you that..."

He bent down and was now connected with my ear causing me to jump a little but I remained calm. "That was supposed to be my baby," he whispered causing me to catch the chills. "I should snap ya fuckin' neck man."

I had tears in my eyes and I truly felt sick to my stomach cause I didn't know how much longer I could stay here. Like, my best friend in the whole world's nigga was secretly in love with me. "Swain." My lips trembled as I looked in the corner of my eye making sure Tricia wasn't coming. "Please don't trip in this girl's house."

He chuckled like it was funny, "you see that girl in there? That's my baby... and I wont disrespect her. She the kind of woman that I need in my life but I cant help what I feel for yo' sour patch ass. I'mma pray to God everyday that he remove that shit. Good luck on yo' baby. And when you get a chance.... apologize to my bitch, and I mean it."

I swallowed hard, "yeah... aiight." I mumbled.

A few seconds later he was heading in the room with Tricia leaving me alone to think the shit over but fuck it, my decision was made and what I did, I couldn't take back. I sat back and placed my hand on my stomach not being able to help the smile that crept across my face because I'd been wanting this for a while and I knew I'd be a good mommy to my precious baby. I felt some type of way about the bad news that Tricia shared with me but in due time she'd get over it and my baby would bring both of us joy. As far as Gu... well, he'll be aiight eventually but like I originally planned. I was gonna stay away from his ass. I knew his cousin had recently been buried so I was gonna give him some time to get over it and then I was gonna just handle shit up on my own.

~~~~~~

"You're six weeks on the head." My doctor told me smiling at my ultrasound amazed by the little peanut sized fetus that I was looking at on the screen. I nod my head in awe as the warm tears threatened to fall from the sides of my eyes. Wiping the cold gel from my belly, she allowed me to sit up and get myself together. After giving me my copies along with a shit load of instructions as far as what foods to stay away from and etc... and after being in there so damn long I was well ready to go. I hated the fact that I didn't have my own whip to get around but I was more than grateful that even after the fight Tricia and me had, she was still sitting in the waiting area waiting for me to come out like a true friend although we barely spoke a word to each other.

"You ready?" She asked me standing up. I simply nod my head and followed her out to the car and hopped in the passenger seat.

The whole ride to the house she hadn't said much to me so I decided to be the bigger person. "Tricia... about the other night, I really didn't mean anything by it. I apologize."

Focusing on the road, she wouldn't even look at me, "well I'm not sorry for slapping the shit out of you. And while I am pissed about how you tricked that man into impregnating you. I apologize for not telling you that I found out I couldn't have kids."

"When did you find out?"

"About a year ago after trying so hard and still not being successful."

That hurt to even hear that she hid that shit from me outta all people. "Why didn't you tell me about it?"

"I was embarrassed RaRa... just leave it alone!" I could tell she didn't wanna talk about it so I wasn't gonna force her. "And you need to tell that man the truth."

I shook my head adamant about my decision, "nah... cause he's gonna make me kill my baby or kill me one. You don't know how crazy Gu really is."

She lightly chuckled, "oh yes the fuck I do. I remember he beat poor Ralph to a fucking mush for fucking him outta some money. I remember he shot the whole damn basketball court up in the middle of a game to confront Tron about eye fucking his lil sister... I remember hearing a couple of niggas came up missing just for disrespecting him and shit. I heard a lot more gruesome stories that I don't even care to think about right now since my breakfast is still sitting heavy in my belly and I don't want it to come up."

"So you get my drift then right? That nigga will kill me if I tell him now. But once I'm big and pregnant and I can't even have an abortion, he wont fuck with me and he wont have no choice but to accept it."

She turned on our block shaking her head, "I really don't like the shit you doing but as your friend I gotta have your back regardless so all I'ma say is I hope you know what you're doing and I'm gonna be there for you and the baby as much as I can."

"Aww that's why I love you Tricia... always got my back." I playfully reached over to hug her.

She gently pushed me back while giggling... "nah bitch I'm still not one hundred percent ready to be buddy buddy wit'cho ass. I'm still debating about slapping the shit out of that other cheek."

I fell out laughing, "nah... wont go down this time baby. That was a first and a last."

My last comment fell on deaf ears as she focused on a pretty exotic looking bitch at the stop sign in Gu's car. I couldn't lie, she looked damn good sitting in the driver seat of his tricked out Camaro but who the fuck was she?

"That's the girl I was telling you I saw with Gu the day his mama them was having that fish fry before Ronnie's funeral." Tricia informed me.

I felt a pain in my gut and a twitch of jealousy cause this nigga had never let me drive his fucking car. "Fuck that bitch... cause when he finds out about our baby he gonna be right over here with me and that punk ass hoe gonna be gone."

"A baby don't keep no nigga tho RaRa."

I didn't wanna hear that shit there, cause Hennessy's baby sho kept him running back to her ass so I was gonna play my cards right and make him see why he should be a family with me and our child. "Fuck that... take me home." I said with much attitude just as the bitch hit the corner riding right past us without a care in the world and not oblivious to us even sitting there staring at her. I couldn't wait to bust they fucking bubble.

Tricia sighed, "I wont even say nothing else about it. Let's go show Swain our little nugget cause I know he gonna spoil this baby just as much as me."

I felt a way in the pit of my stomach when she said that but I dared not say anything about it. I closed my eyes and rest my head back until we arrived. At this point I wasn't gonna let shit stress me and my baby out.

Chapter 5

Messiah (Gu) Carter

"I love you Messiah! I love youuuu!" Hennessy moaned just as I dropped the last bit of my nut into the slippery condom that protected us both. The pussy was good and I may have been drunk when I got here, but not drunk enough to not strap the fuck up. I didn't want no more kids and no more baby mama's... especially if they was gon' be aggravating like Hennessy's ass for no damn reason. I knew it was my fault that I kept digging in the pussy but this time it really wasn't on me. Beans them knew that I'd been down bad since we buried Ronnie and my only relief was turning to the bottle.

After a drunk ass night of gambling and smoking, I told them niggas to drop me off to the crib since I didn't have my whip, and instead they chose to drop me to Hennessy's house since we were closer to her hood. All a nigga wanted to do was sleep and after getting some rest for a couple of hours, Hennessy was practically putting the pussy in my face on a platter. Woke me up with some mean, sloppy ass head like a bitch from a porn. She knew exactly how to get me in order to get what she wanted. I usually didn't like to trip like this if my daughter was home cause I couldn't live with myself if she ever walked in on us but since she was with Sue, I gave her just what she was looking for and since I wasn't fuckin' with RaRa... a nigga was backed up anyway.

"Where you going?" Hennessy followed me to the bathroom watching me hop in her shower.

"I gotta go home and then I gotta go grab Winter and take her out for the day." I answered trying to be as patient as possible with her while she stood there butt ass naked looking like a whole meal with her fine ass.

"You don't love me no more Messiah... tell the truth."

I knew she couldn't wait to get me in her presence where I couldn't run and couldn't hang up the phone in order for her to continue the conversation she'd been trying to have with me. I let the steam hit my body and washed off so I can get the fuck outta the hot seat. A nigga didn't have time for this shit here at all. "How many times I gotta tell you I love you Nessy? The fuck you want me to say man? I really be tryna be patient with yo feelings but you just don't get it."

"Why aren't you in yo car Gu?"

"Why you in my business Nessy?" I frowned now hopping out drying off. Personally I didn't think it was none of her business as into where or why I didn't have my car. Ever since they stripped Turquoise for her lil ride, a nigga felt bad for the girl and I let her use my Camaro on a couple occasions to go to school while I handled my shit driving around in my lil bucket... my spare whip. But last night I told Turquoise to just hold it down till I got back to the hood and she agreed. I didn't mean for her to keep my shit overnight, but again, it was Beans them fault for not taking me the fuck home. Now I was stuck to deal with this shit. "A friend got my car."

"As in girlfriend?" She snapped.

"Man." I exhaled tryna keep it together, "did I say that?"

"I'ma move on Messiah... I got to." She said with tears in her eyes. "Cause if I don't, this shit gonna kill me."

Pulling my clothes back on, I argued within' myself cause I was just as wrong as her. Every time I told myself I wouldn't touch her, some kind of way I end up being right back in the pussy and every single time she acted worse than the last. It was true what they say... a nigga can fuck a female with no emotions attached but a female couldn't do that kind of shit... at least not a female like Hennessy. I asked myself over and over if I could deal with her or my daughter being around another nigga, but in actuality, it was selfish of me to even feed her peanuts of feelings just to keep a nigga from being around them.

"You know what Nessy? I can't even be mad at you right now cause I know this shit is wrong and I can man up to that. It ain't right for me to keep doin' this shit. I know it ain't so I'mma be a man and apologize. I promise you this was the last time and I wont play these games with you no more." I gently grabbed her chin and forced her to look at me on some sentimental shit, some shit I wasn't used to but I needed her to understand how real this shit was. She tried to look away. "Nah, look at me man... forreal Nessy. In any way possible I wanna be there for you and Winter but I don't wanna do nothin' that's gon' keep hurting you so this shit gotta stop and it's gon' stop today."

I hated watching her lips trembling as she tried to gather the words but this shit was long overdue and it needed to happen. I wasn't no lying ass nigga and I didn't sugarcoat shit. The only reason I ever tried to tiptoe around Nessy's feelings is cause she was my child's mother and we had history... that don't mean it made it right tho. Pushing back from me, she nod her head. "Aiight... I understand. This how it gotta be and this how it should've been long ago. You can let yo'self out Messiah. I have to make a run." She walked away leaving me alone. I guess she went in her room to put on some clothes cause not too long after, I heard the keys dangling and the door slamming. That was the hardest shit to do... but the shit had to be done or neither one of us would've ever been able to move forward.

As soon as I was finished dressing I called Beans to come and grab me since I didn't wanna have Turquoise pulling up at my BM house and shit. "Nigga, why the fuck you green ass niggas drop me off here? I said take me to the fuckin' crib man." I went in on his ass soon as I sat in the driver seat of his whip.

With a fat ass joint to his mouth, he laughed like I was fuckin' jokin' and I didn't see a fuck thing funny. "Nigga you act like the bitch raped you." He teased.

"Yo Beans... on the real, you my nigga but that's still my baby mother. Watch yo' fuckin' mouth B." I warned.

He exhaled and then passed me the much needed joint, "you right... my bad fool you know we respect the BM's and shit. But what happen?"

"Nothing man.... She just a real bug sometime but I'd be lying if I said I didn't love the girl cause I do. I just can't go backwards."

"What you mean?"

"Exactly what I said... nigga me and Nessy had that young love but we just ain't no good for each other no more. We don't mix man... that shit is a disaster waiting to happen so why even bother, ya feel me?"

"Awe don't be like that my nigga... you and Nessy been goin' through it since we was in school... you might as well marry the girl."

I looked at him like he was stupid as shit, "you marry the crazy bitch."

"I thought we couldn't refer to her as no bitch." He said confused. "Nigga make up yo' mind."

"Nah... that's my baby mother so I can call her what the fuck I want when she pisses me off but you niggas better always show some respect. Disrespecting her is like disrespecting me cuz... and I'm not havin' that." I let him know. Niggas always thought they could get away with some shit if you let em.

Beans crazy ass shook his head again high as a kite, "Yo you bipolar as fuck but I'ma leave that shit alone."

"Yeah... okay." I shrugged. "What's good with you and Monica?"

Immediately he looked aggravated as he hit the joint, "I don't fuckin' know no more my dude. Monica's been on some other shit lately and to be honest with you I think she slidin' out on me... I can't catch her ass but I ain't no fool."

"Get the fuck outta here." I laughed cause everybody in the hood knew her quiet ass was all about Beans and did whatever he said. "Her quiet ass?"

"Shit, them be the ones fam... it be the quiet ones and the preacher's daughters. Them the most freakiest, sneakiest bitches on earth." He said just as we pulled in front of my building.

He did make hella sense though so it wasn't shit I could say.

"What up with the lil chick Qui that been holding the whip? You ain't ever did no shit like that fam." He said calling me out... I can't front cause I knew that shit was coming. I honestly didn't know what it was about Qui's ass. Like I felt sorry for her and all but besides that... she just seemed... I don't know.... Different.

"You know I told you all about how shit played out that night... I just felt sorry for her man. Chick got a good shoulder on her head but she in a fucked up situation. I felt bad about them niggas strippin' her lil whip down on death row and I damn sho wasn't about to be her chauffer everywhere so I let her use it to go to class."

Beans was sitting there giving me the 'get the fuck outta here look' "no bullshit." I chuckled. "I was suppose to do some real damage to her ass before I actually met her. Like I was gon' torture her ass... make her wish she was dead by the time I finished if it was gon' get her to talkin' but it just didn't happen like that."

"Nigga you done got weak."

"Fuck you... " I said before unlocking the door lightly using the back of my hand to tap his chest. "I'mma get up wit'chu later on. I gotta run in here and get Winter from Sue then get my whip from Qui so I can take Winter out for the day.... Nigga tryna be on his daddy shit today."

"I ain't mad at'cha my dude. Hit me when you done and tell lil princess uncle Beans said hey. I'mma go check Cortez real quick and make sure that nigga good." He told me referring to our other homeboy who was more like a brother to us.

"Aiight... and tell that nigga I'mma pull up on em when I drop baby girl back off to her mama... one."

~~~~~~

"Sue!" I called my ole bird name walking through the door of her apartment expecting to be greeted by Winter like she normally did whenever she heard me walking through her grandma's door. She didn't answer me so I walk to her room door figuring that her and Winter was probably taking a nap. It was weird as fuck to see her door closed. "Sue!" I knocked being greeted with the sounds of her and Tuff behind the door.

"Ohhh smack it baby! Right there!" Sue moaned loud enough for me to hear her.

The fuck? If this wasn't some disrespectful as shit I didn't know what the fuck was. How this nigga was gon' be in here fuckin' Sue with my daughter right in the fuckin' room. I started to pull out my gun and just blow the damn lock off the door but I couldn't take a chance like that with Winter in there. Fuck it.

BOOM! BOOM! BOOM!

I turned around and used the back of my size 11's to beat on the door hearing scuffling coming from the other side.

"What the fuck! Who the fuck is it!" Sue yelled swinging the door open butt ass naked under the towel she had wrapped around her body. Tuff lay on the bed with the sheet over him ready to light a blunt. All I saw was red pushing pass Sue ready to jump all over his ass. "Winter ain't here Messiah!" She yelled pulling on me.

"The fuck you mean she ain't here?" I frowned still scolding Tuff.

"Relax nigga' I know what you thinkin'." He said cool as ever like he just wasn't up in here fuckin' my mama. Like I get it, they were both technically young in their late 40's and I know she was gonna do her but that didn't mean I wanted to hear him beating her fuckin' back out.

"Man, where Winter at?" I asked again.

"Her mama came and got her bout ten minutes ago Messiah." Sue rolled her eyes clutching the towel closer to her body. "Didn't Hennessy tell you?"

I furrowed my brows ready to punch a fuckin' wall out. This was the dumb shit with her that I was talkin' about. "Nah she didn't tell me shit... I just left her ass and she knew I was comin' to get Winter."

Sue shook her head, "well I don't know what you did to the girl but she said it'll be a long time before you see Winter again."

"What'chu talkin' bout Sue?" I asked confused like a muthafucka.

"Exactly what I said Messiah."

"And you just let her take her?" I asked.

She threw her hands in the air, "what the fuck was I supposed to do Messiah? That's HER baby! I raised my kids and I'm not fighting with nobody over their kid no matter how much I may love her. Shit when she gets outta her feelings she'll come around. I been told you to stop fucking that crazy ass girl! I love Hennessy and all but this ain't my fucking business."

My nostrils flared thinking about how I was gon' wrap my fuckin' hands around Hennessy's little ass neck and strangle her ass if she kept playin' these punk ass games with me bout my daughter. "Man this some bullshit!"

Tuff shook his head and I already know what he wanted to say cause he'd been telling me forever that if I wanted to have a healthy co-parenting relationship with Hennessy then I had to stop sliding dick in her... yeah yeah yeah... I got it. "Gu, man I keep telling you that shit ain't gone ever work if you don't put a end to that shit." He told me.

"And that's what I did... and look what she did, ran over here to get my daughter and now she wanna keep her away from me. This the shit I be talkin' about man; I ain't no deadbeat ass nigga, I own up to mine... period."

"It's a better way nigga... I see the look in yo eyes. Don't go fuck with that girl. Take her ass to court and do it the right way cause I'm tellin' you... I'm not bonding you out of jail. You gon' learn to take some of my advice one day Gu." Tuff told me while smoking on his joint causing me to frown.

"Tuff... I appreciate that and all but I'm not finna have this sentimental ass convo with you while you up under some silk sheets butt ass naked man." I shook my head. "I'mma hit you up later so we can finish this."

He gave me a simple head nod, meanwhile Sue pushed my ass out slamming the door behind me so she could finish her lil session I guess. As soon as I made it to the front door Bari was walking in. "What's wrong wit'chu?" I asked noticing the visible attitude on her face.

She sucked her teeth, "nothing Messiah, or at least not nothing I wanna talk to you about."

"It's like that Belcalis? As much as I done been there for you?" I felt some kind of way bout that shit. Like the more she grew up the more her lil personality changed.

I saw she felt bad cause her expression changed a lil bit. "I'm sorry Messiah, it's not like that, I'm just stressed."

"About what?" I didn't understand what the fuck a sixteen year old had to be stressed about. She didn't have to do shit besides go to school. Didn't pay not one fuckin' bill and stayed in my pockets for some money.

She sighed, "It's just girl stuff. Where's mama?"

"Ohhh. Um yeah I can't help you with that but Sue a lil busy right now." I told her.

"Doing what?"

"She in there with Tuff."

She immediately stomped off, "stop lying Messiah."

The fuck I had to lie about that for?

I watched Bari walk to the door and place her ear to the door to listen for a few seconds before she walked away. "I'm so sick of this shit!" she yelled in a high squeal. Meanwhile, I'm wondering what kind of weirdo shit she was on.

"Sick of what?" I asked.

"Her! Him! Both of them bitches!" She fumed grabbing her house keys.

I grabbed her arm, "yo Bari you gettin' way out of line lately baby girl. Now if it's something bothering you and you can't talk to me or nobody else about it then I'll pay for you to talk to somebody... but what you not gonna do is be around here doin' this weird shit you doin'."

Her breathing changed slow and steady all-of-a-sudden but before she could respond to me, Becka was walking through the door. "Sue cooked?" She asked wearing a shimmering one-piece bodysuit like she was going to audition for a fuckin' dance show.

"Becka..." Bari's lips trembled. "Can you come take a walk with me?" she pleaded.

Becka ignored my presence being that she always had a weakness for Bari and made her way to her instead. "Aww, what's wrong precious?"

Bari looked from me to Becka like she didn't wanna say. "What? You can't talk in front of me?" I asked.

Bari ignored me again and whispered to Becka, "boy problems."

I acted like I didn't even hear that shit, it was time for me to go so that's what I did. Pulled a hundred dollar bill from my pocket, passed it to Bari and went on my way to Turquoise apartment to get my keys.

~~~~~~

All I heard from the outside of Qui's door was a bunch of fussing on the other side and I recognized her and her sister's Rain voice going back and forth. I didn't have time for this shit... I had my own shit to handle so I didn't even hesitate to knock on the door. Within' a matter of seconds Qui was at the door with tears in her swollen red eyes. Now normally shit didn't bother me like that, but seeing the hurt behind her eyes made me feel some kind of way. "You okay?"

Her eyes bounced around with embarrassment as she cleared her throat, "Um-Gu- I um..." she stopped and grabbed my key from the table by the door shoving them in my face "Here's your keys... thanks again." She tried to close the door.

Using my foot, I blocked it. "Nah lil mama... I'm not leavin' here until you tell me you good."

"I just had a bad argument with Rain... I'm okay though." She said through her tears. Something was up with her and I was gon' get to the bottom of that shit.

"Where ya sister at now?"

Peeking over her shoulder, she turned back to me and shrugged. "In her room now."

I nod my head still looking in her pretty ass eyes. Even with the tears they were still beautiful. In just a matter of seconds my mind was telling me 'fuck that shit' Qui wasn't my girl and this wasn't my problem. I didn't let females get too close to me but it was something about her. I found myself gently grabbing her hand and she quickly snatched away. I grabbed it again. "When I'm tryna to show you some affection... don't deny me lil mama. We homey's and homey's can talk about anything aiight? So stop tellin' me you okay when we both know you really ain't. Come take this ride with me... I'mma be in the car waiting." With that I simply turned my back and walked away from her making my way to the car in the parking spot reserved for my shit only cause everybody knew not to park there.

"You brand new now?" I immediately recognized Meka's voice and wished I'd took the other way around. Meka was bad as fuck... looks... body and all that but I couldn't fuck with her no more. We had a lil somethin' a few years back but she fucked that up when she decided to go befriend RaRa and a nigga like me didn't play those kinda games period. That's how females got a nigga all cased up. She had the prettiest grey 'cat like' eyes that I'd ever seen in my life and her thick ass thighs stood out first under her tiny jean Minnie skirt. She had a big red rose on her right thigh and she rocked a pair of crisp white Air Force Nikes with the matching shirt tied up behind her back. Meka was known for rocking her hair in all the latest cornrow styles and today was no different. Of course she had her signature lollipop in her mouth... wasn't one time I saw her and she wasn't sucking on one.

"What up Meka?" I asked looking up at the staircase noticing Turquoise walking down with some pink UGG boots on her feet. She had on a pair of tights and a wife beater with her long faux locks thrown in a high bun.

Licking her lips, Meka stepped closer... I didn't bother backing up just so I could look her dead in her eyes and tell her what I wanted to tell her.

"I heard you and RaRa don't fuck around no more."

"True."

"So when you gon' let me taste you again?"

"Never... I don't give a fuck about all that Meka. I mean, the pussy was good and all but you crossed all lines befriending RaRa... now I can't fuck with you period."

She sucked her teeth, "Awe me and Ra ain't even rockin' like that right now Gu."

I looked over my shoulder to see that my lil mama finally made it to the passenger side of the car so I hit the unlock button. "Get in... I'm comin'."

Expressionless, she did as she was told. I turned back to Meka. "Like I was sayin' I'm good off you. I don't fuck around in the same camp Meka." I bent down in her ear and whispered. "Yo lost."

I knew she had an attitude, but I didn't give a fuck, I could care less. Right now, I needed to see what was up with Qui and if it was anything I could do to help. Leaving her standing there, I hopped in the car and backed out. Lil mama looked like she was still out of it. "You cold?" I asked her.

"Nah..." she said dryly.

"Hungry?"

She shrugged, "a little."

I stopped at the stop sign and put the car in park. "You sure you okay lil mama?"

"Gu I'm fine."

"So why you still crying then?" I used the back of my forefinger to wipe her tears watching her close her eyes like she was savoring my touch. Shit was sexy to me the way she closed her eyes and took a light deep breath.

Opening her eyes, she finally looked at me. "Gu I'm not tryna be rude or nothing... but why you even care?"

"Would you prefer that I didn't? Would you prefer that I acted like you didn't even exist? Or better yet, how would you have felt if I'd come to the door and didn't even acknowledge all the hurt that I saw in yo eyes, how would you feel?"

"Nobody ever cared about me Gu. And you barely even know me."

"So what that mean?" I asked.

"I don't know Gu..."

"Look, I saw the love both yo parents have for you so be appreciative of that shit cause most muhfuckas in the hood that I come from... they parents don't give a fuck about em. Ion even know my real daddy and neither does my sister. All we had was our mama and she did the best she could... so nah... somebody loves you."

"Rain don't love me though." She sniffed.

"Lift ya head up ma... she'll come around... don't ever let nobody see you down and show ya weakness unless it's yo man... cause he probably the only one that can make it better." I said giving off a light smile hoping to lighten her mood a little.

It worked and I knew it did when I saw her force a tiny smile on her exotic looking face. It was crazy, like... the structure of her facial bones and everything else was sexy as fuck. "I wanna eat waffle house." She told me.

"Aiight, what lil mama wants... lil mama get."

"You ever gon' stop callin' me that?"

"Till the day you become Mrs. Carter." I told her focusing on the road.

That got a real good laugh outta her, "is that yo last name?"

"Betta know it... Messiah Carter... remember me."

"You got so much game Gu."

"Is it workin'?"

She giggled even more, "yes."

"That was the plan baby... now lets go get these waffles and shit you tryna stuff a nigga with." Just in this little time, she was helping me even escape my problems and she didn't even know it. Being in her presence alone right now was refreshing as hell. When we got to the Waffle House I watched her in disbelief as she gobbled down one whole waffle, pan sausage, grits, eggs, and toast swallowed by a cup of orange juice. "Shit lil mama... you hungry?" I asked in all seriousness. "I mean, I can order some more if you want me to."

"No silly... I haven't eaten in two days Gu." She informed me using a napkin to wipe her mouth.

"Why not?"

"Stress..."

Damn, was it just me or were all the women in my life stressed the fuck out? Bari had said the same thing a few hours earlier. I leaned forward and pulled my phones out putting them on silent and then I sat both phones in the middle of the table.

"What you doing?" Qui asked me.

"You got my undivided attention lil mama... I'm all ears... no phones no nothin' now tell me what's wrong?"

She tried to brush me off, "it's not important."

I raised a brow. "So you sayin' you not important?"

"No... that's not what I'm saying. I'm just saying you don't have to do all of that. It's not even worth all that." She said all that refusing to look at me.

"Look at me." I told her.

Her eyes shift and landed on me briefly, "you make me nervous Gu."

"Forget all that Qui... you don't think you worth that?" I asked.

"I guess so..."

I grabbed both her soft hands and examined the fresh pink and white manicure. I was a sucker for a chick with nice hands and feet. It was the bitches with the chipped and cracked nail polish that was a problem. "You don't know you a queen? Act like it... ain't no 'I guess so'. You know for somebody so smart you don't think a lot of yo'self?"

"Gu... I don't even know myself." She said almost in a whisper.

"Now we gettin' somewhere... you right, I don't understand so help me to understand. I'm listening."

She sighed and took another deep breath. "When I was fourteen Rain and I had our parents car. She let me drive and we ended up getting into a bad accident. I woke up six months later in a coma and didn't remember shit about my life up until that point. I went through therapy for an entire year after that. It's like I was reborn or something... like given a new fresh life to start over. But you can't imagine how it feels to feel like I don't even know myself. I don't even know the real reason my own blood sister hates me more than she loves me. I don't know what kind of relationship we had prior to that but it sucks that I just can't remember... I just can't." She choked up on tears and I let her cause she needed this... she needed to get it all out. "After therapy I continued on with school and I was able to work really hard to catch up and graduate on time. I moved out a few months ago and now this is where I am... in college and working a little pizza job in the meantime."

"You strong lil mama... real strong." I told her feeling like I'd known her for years just from that lil bit that she gave me. "God gives his toughest battles to his strongest soldiers. Speak it into existence... you gon remember one day and get that peace you lookin' for... and need... and I'ma be with you every step to help wherever I can."

She wiped a tear from her eye. "But why Gu?"

I told her straight up, "cause I care."

"Besides my parents the only other person that cared about me was Rain's ex-boyfriend Butta and he's dead."

"Well now you can add Messiah 'Gu' muhfuckin' Carter to that list."

She was laughing again, which made me happy. I really didn't know what it was about this chick but she wasn't like the hood rats from the block. She was makin' me soft... had me feelin' like a gook and shit. "Okay Mr. Carter.... I hear you."

"Let me ask you somethin' else...."

"What is it?" she questioned sipping on her lemonade.

"That night you was with me..."

She cut me off, "you mean the night you kidnapped me?"

I chuckled and lightly stroke my goatee, "if that's what you wanna call it... but look, I meant to ask you that night. Why don't you like hotels?"

She looked uncomfortable again, "I really don't know, I can't remember. It's not that I don't like them Gu... I'm really scared of them shits. I hate them and I don't know why. I get a feeling in the pit of my stomach every time I even think I have to go in one. You would've surely killed me that night because I wasn't going in Gu."

This shit was starting to fuck with me and it wasn't even my situation. "You gon' be aiight lil mama... I promise you. I'ma make sure of that."

She squint her eyes like something was on her mind.

"Talk to me." I told her.

"It's nothing.... Really." She tried to shy away from answering but she was gon' learn I wasn't that type of nigga. If I told a female she didn't have to be afraid to talk to me about nothing, that's exactly what I meant.

"Don't do that shorty.... Wus good?"

Looking at me sideways she spoke up. "What exactly did you plan on doing to me that night? I heard things about you Gu. I did my research and you're not as innocent as you look. You're definitely not a force to be reckoned with."

The waitress put the bill on the table and walked away. I pulled out a fifty-dollar bill and sat it on the table. "I rather not say cause then you may not ever wanna come around me... you ready?" I asked her.

"I guess..." she chuckled scooting out of the booth. I made sure I opened the door to let her out and then opened her car door before she got in.

"What's all this for?"

"Like I said... I'm surrounded by women in my life and I always dedicate myself to make sure I can make you feel better." I closed the door and walked around to the driver side.

"Are you referring to other females as in bitches you fuck with?" she asked as soon as I sat down and crank the car up.

"Maybe..." I shrugged. "But nah, on some real shit I have a family full of females. Like I pay all my mama bills and my auntie too. I make sure my granna is good and even my lil sis and my baby mother and daughter. Trust me they all drive me crazy sometime but I do the best I can, even when they give me a flat out attitude."

She slowly nod her head, "hmmm, I see. So what exactly do you do Gu? And if you pay everybody bills then why do they still live in the hood? Like why didn't you get them a house like you did your lil sister?"

I hit the corner on 22nd Ave and headed to Hennessy's house... I bet she thought I forgot about the lil stunt she pulled but I had a trick for her ass. Focusing back on my convo with Qui, I couldn't help but laugh. "First off, I don't know why females always asking niggas what kind of work they do... it don't even matter... as long as I get my money and keep everybody outta my business. A man's job is to take care of his family and I make sure it's done. Second, my mama and my auntie them don't wanna leave the hood and that aint my fault. Hell, that's all they know and if they don't want better I cant force them but in the meantime, I'm still gonna pay whatever bills they have... I don't give a fuck if it is subsidized housing. Now my lil sis, that's something different... that's my baby right there so if I can make it happen for her to leave the hood and not have the same mentality as my mama and my auntie than that's what I'ma do."

"How old is your daughter?"

"She three and her name is Winter." I told her and normally I didn't really talk to females about my daughter, she was off limits.

I saw a twinkle in her eyes when I told her that, "Awww..." she gushed. "That's a blessing."

"Thanks." I was waiting for her to start bombarding me with questions about my baby mother like any other female would've done but it never happened. The only person she was concerned with was Winter.

"Can I see a picture of her?"

I pulled out my phone and showed her my screensaver.

"OMGGGGG." She gushed. "She's beautiful Gu... and look at all that hair! She looks exactly like you, only a light skin version."

"Yeah, Hennessy is mixed."

She furrowed her brows, "Hennessy?"

"Yeah, that's my baby mother name."

"Her government? You bullshittin'." She laughed.

"Nah... G-shit."

One look at her face and we were both sharing a friendly chuckle. "It's different." She said.

"Yep... and so is she." I said.

We were almost to Hennessy's house by now and she started to say something else but her phone rung. I couldn't help but to glance over and look at the name on the screen. *Hulk?* I said to myself knowing that was a dude name. Then it hit me, all this talkin' and I never asked the girl if she had a man.... But then again, if she had one then why the fuck wasn't he goin' over and beyond to make sure she got to school and was tryin' to keep a smile on her face? Nah fuck that... if that was her nigga I was about to give him a piece of my mind like *'nigga where the fuck yo antennas been for the past couple of weeks?'*

Before she could answer I hurriedly grabbed the phone from her hand shocking her. "What the hell are you doing?" she raised her voice catching a fit. I really needed to see if she was gon' fight me for this phone. If she fought me like a nigga in the streets to make sure I didn't answer this muthafucka, then I knew this was definitely her man or a nigga she was fuckin' but when she didn't, and sat there looking at me crazy instead... I passed it back to her.

"Thought that was ya nigga or somethin'." I said. "My bad."

She rolled her eyes and answered on speakerphone. "Hey Hulk."

"Hey dawlingggg." He sang.

The fuck kind of gay ass shit was that?

"Hey Hulky." She cooed.

Oh God it got worse.

"You seemed zoned out in class the other day chica... what happened to you?" he asked. I could tell off rip he was a white boy.

"Yeah, I know... I was just in a bad headspace but I'm getting over it now."

"I totally understand.... I've been having some man problems myself." He told her.

Awe shit... now here go the bullshit.

Her eyes stretched in shock when he said that. "You have a boyfriend Hulk? You're gay?" she gasped.

He chuckled, "well yeah Edwards... I just don't go around school telling my business."

"But Hulk... you bring me pastries and orange juice every other day. On holidays and my birthday you always buy me expensive and over the top gifts..."

"And what does that mean Edwards? I love you as a friend... and I'm a damn good friend to have. It didn't mean I wanted to swim in the fish market." He laughed.

"OMGGGG.... How embarrassing." She covered her mouth.

I looked at her shaking my head while mocking dude on the phone. Qui playfully hit my arm and continued focusing on Hulky or whatever the fuck his name was.

"Don't even worry about it Edwards... I wanted to know what were your plans for your birthday? It's two weeks away and you haven't said anything."

Hmmm, that was interesting cause she hadn't mentioned shit about a birthday to me either. "Don't worry! She ain't tell me shit either!" I yelled loud enough for him to hear me.

"Oh My Jesus!" he gasped. "You're with a guy right now Edwards? I want to know all the details! Are you gonna let him be the first to pop the cherry?" He asked excited.

Qui's face was flushed with pure embarrassment! A nigga like me was shocked too. *A virgin?*

"WOWWW HULK!" She rushed him off the phone "I'll call you later!"

"But wait Nooooo! We have to talk boys." He pleaded while laughing.

"Hulk... bye!" she hung up on him now looking out the window instead of at me. I could tell she was embarrassed so I didn't bother to ask her about it although that shit was a definite plus. You know how hard it was to find purity now days? I knew for sure I was locking her ass in.

"Where are we?" She asked when we pulled up in front on Nessy's duplex. The brand new 2017 Nissan Maxima that 'I' purchased for her ass sat in the front clean and sparkling and that shit bothered me even more. How dare her try to keep my daughter away from me... all the shit I did for her ass.

"Do me a favor Qui... it's a corner store right around the corner. Go to the stop sign and make a right and you'll see it. I gotta handle some business aiight? Wait there and I'll call you in a few."

"Ummm, okay but I think I need some kind of protection if I'm gonna be doing all that Gu. Last corner store I was at I got caught slipping and you got my ass." She shook her head. "Nope, never again."

Lil mama put a smile on my face with that one. She was gon' be aiight with me. I just knew it. "It's a 9 in the glove compartment and ain't no safety on it. You'll be good though, this area is decent." I wouldn't have had it any other way for my baby girl... she needed to be safe at all times and I didn't want her living in the hood. "Go ahead." I told Qui as she backed out and I didn't walk away until I saw the taillights hit the corner. It was time to pay my conniving ass baby mother a visit.

Chapter 6

Hennessy 'Nessy' Morales

"Mommy do I get to-to see my daddy?" Winter asked as I bathed her little body in the tub watching her splash the fresh bubbles around and play with her floating rubber duckies with tears glossed over in my eyes trying desperately to hide them from her.

I grab the soft rag and put a little warm water on her back and then tried to finish washing her hair. "Hold still baby... let me make sure all the shampoo is out."

"But mommy... do I get to see him?" She asked again refusing to let up.

"Yes baby... but it won't be soon." I sighed hoping she didn't ask me fifty million questions about it. "Daddy has to work, but he loves you very much."

"But whyyyy." She whined on the verge of crying. I know she loved her daddy and she had every reason to because he loved her unconditionally and had been there for her since day one. Whatever she wanted, she got it. Messiah was the type of daddy who would sit and play dress up with her, or even paint her nails, or do her hair when I was nowhere around to do it even if it was wop sided as the end result. While I was pregnant with Winter, it wasn't not one night that he wouldn't come to my house just to rub on my belly and talk to her. *'My baby gone know her daddy... I don't give a damn'* is something that he would always say. Hell, even when I came home with her from the hospital... Messiah would never let me get up in the middle of the night and feed her, he wanted to literally do everything. Every holiday he even made sure they dressed alike and it was the cutest thing ever... I won't lie... God gave me an awesome baby daddy.

Even now, I didn't have to do shit for her unless I wanted to. Messiah gave me money orders weekly to cover daycare expenses, put food in my house, brought all her clothes, shoes, and everything else. I didn't even need help paying my bills because being that I didn't have to financially take care of Winter, it left me always having a nice bank account but even still... Messiah covered my light bill and water bill on a monthly basis just because his daughter had to live here with me and her wellbeing was his main concern. Yes, I understood that trying to keep her away was wrong as fuck to the third power but what about my feelings? That nigga had me fucked up. I was around before anybody else was around. I gave him his first child, his first girl, and even my virginity; so for him to all of a sudden decide that not only does he wanna stop fucking with me, he was even finally willing to allow me to move on was baffling. It had to be another bitch. I knew Messiah loved me, but I also knew the loved changed and if it wasn't for Winter, he wouldn't be anywhere in the picture. I loved that man beyond LOVE. A love so deep I couldn't even begin to describe and while I may have done a lot of crazy shit to him... I was still a good catch. If he wanted to be done with me then cool but he wasn't about to have unlimited access to his daughter and have another bitch playing 'mommy' to my baby. I don't give a fuck, if I gotta hurt then so does he and at this point the only way I could hurt him was by taking away his most prized procession.

I knew he was gonna be pissed when he found out that I took her but whatever happens was just gonna happen. I even changed the locks on my front door immediately when I got home... wouldn't be no coming in and out whenever he wanted. Fuck him and fuck that. I knew it wasn't fair to Winter either but I'd keep her busy enough to not even think about his ass. "Come on Winter... time to dry off so you can eat." I grabbed the towel and wrapped it around her body so I could walk her to the room.

She rubbed her eyes, "I don't want to eat mommy..."

"Why baby?"

"I want to go to sleep... and then my daddy will be here when I wake up." She said looking into my eyes with her little eyes full of hope. She'd get over it. After rubbing her body down with lotion and reading her a story, she was knocked out cold so I turned on her nightlight and then turned the soundtrack from the movie 'Frozen' on from the Bluetooth I had set up in her room. This girl was spoiled rotten but that wasn't on me, Messiah started that shit and now I was left to finish it. I closed her room door and walked out and sat on the couch to call my good-good girlfriend Monica since she'd been blowing me up ever since I told her my plans.

"Bout time you called me back." She said into the phone without even saying hello first.

"What'chu doing bitch?" I asked balled up on the couch picking my nail.

"Nothing." She giggled. "Trying to see what lie I'm gonna tell Beans now when I decide to get missing tomorrow night."

I shook my head, "you know you quiet bitches be the worst ones Monica? And besides... you just dumb as shit girl. Like I don't even understand why you would wanna cheat on a nigga like Beans... and with who? Cause you still haven't told me yet."

"I can't tell you." She replied all girlish like.

I rolled my eyes, "whatever."

"Anyway, speaking on my shenanigans... let's talk about yours. Trick, do you know Gu is gonna beat yo ass silly when he catches you? That nigga ain't going for you tryna take his seed away from him and you already know that so what's the plan?"

"Girl I don't know yet... all I know is I changed the locks and I haven't figured out the rest. I guess I'll be hiding out and watching my back."

"I think you should really think about this Nessy... I know you hurt but everything you got came from that nigga... don't you know within' the blink of an eye he can take it all away?"

"Oh fucking well... who the fuck cares? All I know is he not about to be playing house with the next bitch when it come to my daughter." I reminded her again since she acted like she didn't get it. I focused on my Pomeranian named 'TuTu' standing by the back door waiting patiently for me to let her outside to use the bathroom. TuTu meant everything to me and although Messiah hated dogs... he made sure he gave me TuTu a little after I had Winter and she's been my other child ever since. Now Winter, on the other hand was just like her dad... she didn't really fuck with TuTu too much but my dog was my baby and I took damn good care of her... she meant everything to me. I grabbed my robe and slipped on my thong slides that were sitting by the back door so I could let her do her thing while still talking to Monica.

"Nessy? You heard what I said girl?" She asked.

"Damn... my bad girl... no I didn't hear you, I was tryna let TuTu out."

"Can't believe you named that damn dog TuTu." She cracked up. I didn't see what was funny, like I said... I didn't play about my dog.

"Girl, whatever." I said closing and locking the backdoor back while TuTu was still out there since she knew not to go too far. I cradled the phone between my ear and shoulder so I could run to the bathroom and pee real quick. When I was finished, I went back to the back patio.

"Let me call you back Nessy... my boo is calling." She told me and I could tell she was cheesing through the phone.

"Um hmm... okay." I hung up scanning the backyard. "TuTu!" I yelled. She knew not to just get missing and right now she wasn't nowhere in sight. I stepped out into the grass a little further trying not to panic "TuTu! Where you at girl?" I found my way near a small bush right next to my mango tree. I had to use the light from my phone since it was so dark out. Hell, she was so damn little I didn't even see her laying there in the grass. I exhaled a sigh of relief and clapped my hands at her. "TuTu what you doing girl?" I giggled. She didn't move. "TuTu?" I stepped closer and my heart dropped along with my knees... my baby wasn't moving. I immediately went to try to pick her up but before I could I was being yanked by my hair and lift to my feet from behind. I didn't even have to turn around to know who it was... I slipped big time.

Messiah looked like a killer and I had only managed to see the look he had in his eyes one time before since I'd known him and that was when he beat the shit outta my uncle for trying to touch on me. Jacking me up by my robe I was literally off my feet with my toes dangling toward the ground with pure fear in my eyes. "You see how you feel about that muhfuckin' dog?" he growled. "That's how I feel about you tryna take my daughter... bitch I'll kill you and have ya body in the bottom of the muhfuckin' rock pit." His eyes were bloodshot red and he looked like he was foaming around the mouth. I was so scared I didn't even realize how much until I felt my own piss trickling down my legs. He looked down and frowned before glazing at me again. "Oh what? You ain't got shit to say now huh?" He gripped tighter... I couldn't breathe. "Regardless of how you feel about me... bitch I'm a good ass father to 'OUR' child... and a damn good baby daddy to yo triflin' ass too. If you think I'ma be one of these weak ass niggas and let you just take my baby from me you got me fucked up. Ask her who she would rather live with bitch! I bet I be the first selection... the best daddy in the world is what she would say."

"Mes—Mess...iahhh." I couldn't breath. I was desperately scratching at his hands and face, but he wasn't faze by the shit at all. He was gripping so tight... my eyes were bulging and I knew for sure I looked like a damn blowfish.

He tilt his head like a crazy man and I couldn't do shit but blame myself for this one. I let my feelings cloud my judgment and forgot how crazy my baby daddy could really be. "Oh wait... you can't breathe?" he chuckled. "Yeah bitch, that's how I felt when I got the word that you was tryna take my daughter from me... and you got me fucked up. See, I always respected you and you took it as a nigga bein' weak now you got me out here treatin' you like a bird since you wanna act like one." He brought his face so close to mine I thought he was about to bite the tip of my fucking nose off as my fresh salty tears burned my eyes. I knew for sure this was it, but when he use his other hand and pulled his gun out and shoved it in my mouth I went buck ass crazy! My bowels instantly loosened as I tried my hardest to squeeze my ass cheeks together to keep the bowel from falling. It was no use... my fucking lace panties didn't stand a chance.

"I'm sor-rrry." I cried, cause I really was. I really underestimated him. It was stupid to play these fucking games. After being satisfied that he put enough fear in me, he allowed me to fall to the ground like a rag doll as I grabbed my neck coughing uncontrollably. Messiah looked down at me like I wasn't shit and that hurt more than anything. I knew I fucked up, big time.

"Tomorrow... I'm comin' for my baby and I'm keepin' her for a week. Play games with me if you want to... next time I'll kill yo ass." He tucked his gun back in the small of his waist and casually walked off like he didn't kill my fucking dog and then cause me to not only piss but shit on myself too. This was too much. I'd never been humiliated like this in my life. It took me another hour to get myself together after showering and everything else and when I did, Messiah had me so shook I didn't even wanna spend the night home. Plus, I was grieving in the worst way... that nigga killed TuTu. I had to get out the fucking house.

~~~~~~

Monica stood at the door of the house she shared with Beans, which wasn't too far from 'Da Nolia' where Messiah them lived. With her hand on her hips she shook her head and ignored me while grabbing a sleeping Winter from my arms. "Shhh." She put one finger to her lips and walked away to go lay my baby down in her room. I took it upon myself to step inside and close and lock the door behind me. When Monica came back down, I was sitting on her couch just waiting and staring off into space.

She plopped down next to me and just stared for a couple of seconds. Monica was beautiful as fuck and it was no other way to describe her besides 'Ciara' cause that's exactly who she looked like and it was easy to mistake her for the singer on any given day. Only difference is Monica may have been a couple of pounds heavier. "Let me see your neck." She used her soft hand to examine the bruises on my neck. On top of that I had a headache out of this world.

"Ouch." I flinched when she touched it.

She sighed and stood up, "let me go get you some alcohol pads." She was only gone for a few seconds before she was back in front of me. "Here..." She sat them in my lap. "I know damn fucking well you didn't think I was about to rub you down... I fucking told you not to play with that man." She frowned.

I held one finger up to stop her ass. "Bitch I didn't come over here for your speech. I came to get the fuck away from my house for the night. You can save the extra shit."

"Humph." She plopped back down. "As long as you know."

I looked at her crazy, "you know, for somebody who barely use to say anything you're getting real bold lately."

"I guess that new dick will do it to you." She shrugged noticing the big black trash bag that was next to my foot. "What's in the bag?" She asked while voluntarily opening before I could answer.

"DON'T!" I blurted. "It's TuTu!"

It was too late; her face was already examining the bag. She dropped it to her feet and ran to the hall bathroom to vomit. By the time she came out, I was walking out to her backyard.

"YOU BROUGHT A FUCKIN' DEAD ASS DOG TO MY HOUSE! BITCH ARE YOU CRAZY! TUTU IS DEADER THAN A MOTHERFUCKER AND YOU BROUGHT THE DEAD BITCH HERE! ARE-YOU-FUCKING-CRAZY!"

I rolled my eyes, "Can you help me bury her please."

"YOU GOT A LOT OF FUCKING NERVE!" She continued to fuss but even with all that, I knew she was gonna help me. "I need a drink." She complained. "I'ma help ya ass cause I know how you felt about this damn dog. Ironically, I don't even wanna know the details cause I'm sure I know what happened."

After I dug a small hole next to her oak tree, she helped me to put the bag with TuTu's little body in it and I cried the whole time. "Thanks Monica." I sniffed.

She wiped her hands on a towel and blew hard. "Why couldn't you do this at yo house?" she shook her head, "anyway you're welcome girl."

When we got back inside, we were greeted with Beans and Cortez fine ass sitting at the dining room table chopping it up about some money moves but they both stopped talking when we walked in. I was immediately embarrassed by my appearance. "Sup ya'll." I spoke softly as Monica walked over to Beans giving him a dry hug and kiss on the cheek. If that bitch was going for an Oscar she'd fail big time cause even 'I' could see it was fake. She was tripping, Beans was fine as fuck. Him and Cortez both were light skinned dudes rocking beards and low cuts with hella swag. They were both medium built and muscular and to anyone that didn't know them... they could've passed for brothers. Hell, she showed Cortez more love when she greeted him then she did her own nigga.

"The fuck happened to you sis?" Cortez asked me.

"Please enlighten us..." Beans followed behind him.

"I'm going to make drinks... would ya'll like anything?" Monica asked all casual playing the perfect housewife roll again. It was crazy how quick she switched that shit up.

"Um before I say anything, can ya'll put the weed out please? My baby is in the house."

Beans put it out immediately, "Awe shit, my niece here? She sleep?" he asked ready to go find her.

"Yep and I don't want her waken up... so please respect it."

"Yo you always in a bad mood." Cortez chuckled.

I rolled my eyes at his ass; I was truly tired of niggas... period! "Déjame solo estúpido. Estoy tratando de explicar."

He and Beans fell out laughing. "Yo don't be comin' up in here talking that Te Celo Taco Bell bullshit. You in a house full of niggas." Cortez chuckled. "But foreal what happened?"

I explained to them everything that happened and when I was done, neither one of them had nothing to say about it. "So ya'll don't have nothing to say?" I asked in disbelief. "Ya'll nosy ass wanted to know so bad now ya'll on mute?"

"Nah sis... I don't get in a man business when it comes to his child... that's on ya'll." Beans replied. Go figure, I knew they'd take up for each other. Monica came out and placed their glasses of Remy on the table and then she passed me a shot of patron.

"Drink this." She told me. I took it to the head and swallowed it in one shot ignoring the burning down my throat and chest. "Here." She shoved hers in my face with her brows furrowed. "Drink mine... you need it more than me." I gladly took hers to.

"Aiight sis... that's enough... you should be good." Cortez put his two cents in.

"Stop calling me 'sis' I'm no longer with Messiah. And that's the problem with you niggas anyway. Ya'll be the main ones, ole cheerleading ass homeboy's. Ya'll be all up in our face calling us 'sis' but will be the first ones to put that nigga on another bitch."

They both hurriedly took their drinks to the head and stood up to leave, not wanting no parts in this. "Well..." Cortez said. "It was nice talkin' to you but we gotta bounce."

"Say Nessy... just chill out aiight. Shit, you may not wanna hear it but you was wrong." Said Beans.

Monica stood off to the side in a daze as I wondered why she wasn't taking up for me like she should've been but it looked like her mind was in a totally different place. "Okay, I was wrong." I shrugged; fuck it.

"Aye Bae..." Beans spoke to Monica as he and Cortez walk to the front door. "I'ma be home late so lock up. I'ma call you and see if you need anything before I get back."

She rolled her eyes behind his back... "Okay."

The fuck was she acting like that? She was pissing me off.

When they were gone, she was talking again. "I'm going to take a shower okay? You gonna be okay?" She asked with sincerity in her eyes.

I shrugged, "go ahead."

While she was in the shower... I sat Indian style on her sofa and was getting mad pissed cause her fucking phone kept going off. It was normal for us to pick up each other's phones and we had each other's passcodes for emergency reasons so I didn't think twice when I opened the text to read it.

From: 305-902-1318: Damn you looked good baby, nigga wanted to fuck the shit outta you right there on the table.

I knew that fucking number and it wasn't Beans. I replayed the number in my head over and over but it didn't take much to put two and two together. This bitch was fucking Cortez. They were slimy as fuck but it wasn't my fucking business. I had my own problems so I closed the phone and laid my ass down.

Chapter 7

Belcalis (Bari) Carter

"Said lil bitch, you can't fuck with me if you wanted to, these expensive, these is red bottoms these is bloody shoes. Hit the store, I can get 'em both I don't wanna choose and I'm quick, cut a nigga off, so don't get comfortable. Ayeeeee!" I rapped along to the lyrics to Bodak Yellow while inside of one of the biggest house parties in 'Da Nolia'. Cardi B was my bitch for so many reasons but the main one was caused we shared the same name, both named Belcalis only difference was her nickname was Cardi and mine was Bari... she was actually Dominican foreal and I wasn't. I don't know what possessed Sue to name me Belcalis... I guess she just had a personal relationship with that name... knowing Sue... who knows?

"Bitchhhh you goin' all the way up tonight huh?" Bambi giggled as we bomb rush them Overtown niggas who were in the building rocking all the latest styles throwing free money all over the place.

"Hell yeah! Fuck that I've been too stressed out... I've been waiting for this night right here!" I yelled over the music still bobbing through the crowd and then stopping to pick up all the money them niggas was throwing. I stood up and stuffed some of it inside of my Tru's hating that I left my purse home but the way these niggas was set up... I didn't wanna carry shit on me that I didn't wanna get snatched. Prepared to walk off again I was greeted with Pete standing right in my face frowning at me.

"Mayne... put that shit down Bari... the fuck you scrambling for dollars for like you a broke bitch or sumthin'?" he scolded me.

"Oooouuuuhhhh!" Bambi hyped the shit up causing me to give her one more look. I didn't know what was up with Pete wanting to be in my business all-of-a-sudden but ever since he played captain save-a-hoe that day.... he'd been trying to be all up in my personal space and in my fucking business.

"What is it to you Pete? Shit, you ain't breaking no bread so why you care?"

"Bruh, yo brother one of the most respected niggas in the hood and you be havin' that man out here lookin' like a damn fool." He looked me up and down. "Yo whole fit probably cost more than half these hoes in here. You got a whole grip on ya feet shorty. What other bitch in here rockin' fucking red bottom sneakers, huh? You tell me?" He act like he was really waiting for an answer. "But you out here scrambling money and shit... get ya shit together mayne." He walked off with his crew as they all low key eyeballed me.

"Humph... guess he told you." Bambi teased but on the real that shit wasn't even funny. Pete had just fucked up my whole mood and vibe. Who the fuck did he think he was?

"Fuck you Bambi." I hissed. "Come stand by the wall with me." We posted on the wall watching the crowd and everybody enjoying themselves. Even Pete's fine ass, which had a bitch grinding all over his dick. Shit pissed me off and although he was up against the wall with one foot propped up and a bottle to his mouth... I still couldn't help but notice him grilling me too.

"You wanna dance?" Some nigga I'd never seen was all in my face all-of-a-sudden trying to get some play.

"No!" I snapped. "Get the fuck outta my face! I wish all you niggas just leave me the fuck alone!

Dude looked like he wanted to cuss my ass out, but instead... he threw both his hands up and backed away from me.

"Don't trip shawty... I'll dance with you." Bambi gave me an evil glare as she clung her hand on to the dudes, whom looked like he was just happy to be getting some play from somebody.

"Whatever." I rolled my eyes.

Bambi leaned over and whispered in my ear, "you need to check yourself bitch... this attitude ain't cute and we'll talk when I get back from doing damage control on yo behalf." She hissed.

Honestly, I didn't give a fuck about none of the shit Bambi was saying cause even as her being my best friend, she couldn't walk a day in my shoes. I understood she was tryna keep clean face with the majority of these niggas since she was the plug in "Da No'.... like literally Bambi had the hook-up on everything and was definitely all about her money. She may have been a little on the ghetto side 'let Messiah tell it' but she was a good person and a true hustler at heart. She didn't have a choice, unlike Sue, who actually did provide and steal and shit for us when we were younger.... Bambi's mama never did shit. Bambi was practically raising herself she didn't have a choice but to get it off the muscle.

I watched her give that weirdo looking nigga she was dancing with the dance of his life before she came back over to me all out of breath and full of laughs. "Look..." She nudged me. "What the fuck you did to Pete that he's still grilling you?"

I didn't even look at his ass... "Who cares."

"You know you like him..."

"And?" I frowned.

"And? Bitch you need to be hooking up with him and leave Tuff's ass the fuck alone Bari... you too young to be stressed... and besides, that's NOT YOUR NIGGA!"

"Yeah well try telling him that shit." I really hated when Bambi spoke like that about Tuff. Like she really didn't understand that we were really one. Fuck Sue! Tuff wasn't her nigga foreal and she couldn't do it like me or he wouldn't have kept coming back to me for some bomb ass sex.

Bambi got serious all-of-a-sudden, "He don't love you Bari."

I shook my head, "nah... he loves me. He just waiting till I get of age so he can tell Sue what the play really is."

We were interrupted by another dude that I didn't know but apparently Bambi did cause he hugged her and she embraced him back. "Damn Bam... nigga been lookin' for you all night. I need a cookie."

She smiled and shook her head, "not tonight Bruce... I don't have nothing on me. Come see me tomorrow though."

"Damn...." He said frustrated. "You know who got a bomb?"

She shrugged. "Try Vic them... they over there by the bar." She pointed. "Just tell'em I sent you."

"Aiight back dat up Bam." He hugged her again.

"Sorry about that." She focused back on me. "I knew I should've brought the weed with me... you know how much a cookie cost?" She complained. "Damn, I slipped."

I chuckled but loved her hustle.

"Anyway, like I was saying... you need to let it go. And besides if Gu finds out... bitch Tuff wont even be around for you to fuck him at all anymore."

My little heart hurt even thinking about such a thing, I think I'd lose it if something happened to my man with his fine ass. "Gu wont find out... but guess what?"

"What?"

"I'm pregnant again." I admitted.

Bambi took a long deep breath, "I can't help you this time Bari." She shook her head disgusted. "This shit is crazy but you on your own with this one."

"I'm not having an abortion." I blurted.

She covered her ears, "I don't care! I don't care! I DO NOT CAREEEE!" She sang agitated. "Keep all the details to yo'self."

I expected Bam to trip but I knew she'd get over it. And I also knew she would help me with whatever I needed too. I caught a glimpse of Pete staring at me again and all-of-sudden I had a plan. It was actually perfect and quite genius. The only way I could have a baby and keep Tuff under the radar was to blame it on somebody else. My mind was made... tonight, I was fucking Pete like my life depended on it cause it really did. I stepped away from the wall forcing myself in his direction. It couldn't be all that bad. I did kind of low key like his ass, he was fine, young, and had his own money. The only problem would be his hoes cause I knew for sure once they got a whiff of me being his baby mother they would be for sure trying to fight me every chance they got but I'd just have to cross that bridge when we got there... tonight, I was on a mission.

"Where you going?!" Bambi asked.

I stopped briefly to tell her she can go ahead and go when she was ready, "Go ahead and leave when you ready! I'm catching a ride with Pete!" I yelled before taking off again. When I got to Pete, another bitch was all up in his face so I politely stepped in between them with my back turned to the girl as I faced Pete. Licking my lips, I made sure I stood with my legs slightly open.

The girl behind me cleared her throat, "Um excuse you..."

I politely turned around and smiled, "you're excused... I need to holla at my man real quick."

"Man?" She questioned.

"Man, I'ma catch up with you in a minute Sharifa..." he told the girl looking at me questionably. "Let me see wussup with her."

The Sharifa girl stomped off with an attitude.

"Hope I didn't ruin your pussy for the night." I shrugged while laughing.

He ignored my sarcasm, "you done collecting niggas money?" He asked

"You done having an attitude and trying to check me?" I replied.

"Bari... you know a nigga been tryna fuck with you but I'm not bout to play these games with you shorty.... What it's gone be?" He asked in all seriousness tired of my shit.

I stepped a little closer in his space licking my lips, "I'm leaving with you."

"Cool..." He said all smooth and shit, "let me make sure my woes good and we can bounce." He grabbed me by the hand and led me through the crowd with him and then he abruptly stopped pushing me to the ground. "GET DOWN!"

I fell but not before I saw him pull his gun out aiming carefully.

Tat! Tat! Tat! Tat!

I knew something was bound to pop off the minute I saw those Overtown niggas in the building. I tried my hardest not get stomped on as I crawled my way back to the wall where it was safe. People were scattering, hoes was screaming, and bullets was flying. It was the war of the East and South in this bitch. "Bari!" Bambi scrambled next to me. "Bitch what the fuck?!" She yelled with her head down. I noticed the back door fly open and a stampede of people broke through trying to get out.

"What the fuck happened!" she asked when we got out.

"Girlllll.... I don't know..." I said with wild eyes, "but this not the place I'm tryna be."

"Me either..." she replied as we both casually took the back way, which led us on death row walking the strip as the cool Miami breeze smacked our faces. I guess we weren't the only ones thinking of taking the back way cause death row was packed all of a sudden and I wanted to get far away from here. A matte black Hummer truck pulled on the side of us with some dark ass tints and we both gave each other one look prepared to take off. The passenger side window rolled down and Pete was sitting behind the wheel.

"Get in!" He ordered. For a nigga in high school he had so much bossiness in him, like he truly moved like a lil young boss and I had to respect that. He didn't even have to tell us twice when he told us to hop in cause on death row wasn't where we were tryna be anyway. Last time I was on death row Pete had to save me from Dro and now here he was saving me all over again.

"Whew!" Bambi exhaled when she slid in the back after we pulled off. "Bet that up Pete."

"Ain't no problem." He replied with his eyes still focused on the road. I noticed a little blood trickling down the side of his face.

Reaching over to examine it, I saw a little gash right by his tapeline. I took a napkin from the middle console and dabbed it for him. He flinched. "Sorry, just let me put a little pressure on it." This time he didn't move.

"You goin' to 'Da No'?" He asked Bambi.

"Yep, I'm in for the night, this too much shit for me in one night."

When we pulled in front of our building, it was still early, only 10 p.m. to be exact. The party had just started and them niggas ruined it. "See you later girl." I told Bambi when she hopped out.

"Um hmm.... See ya'll." She waved and we watched her until she made it up the steps. I felt the vibration of my phone and looked down to see that Tuff was calling me but it was no way I could've answered him right in front of Pete's ass. Plus I was still pissed at him for fucking Sue cause he promised me that the last time was the last time... same shit he said the time before that. In the beginning it was cool but it wasn't fun no more. I knew I was losing my damn mind when I almost blew my own cover in front of Messiah.

"You sure you goin' with me?" he asked before we pulled off.

"Yeah... I'm good." I replied. Even in his face I could tell that he was still mad tight about whatever had popped off back at the party but I was smart enough to know not to ask any questions either. Messiah taught me that part.

~~~~~~

"Who you live here with?" I asked Pete when we got inside of the small efficiency in Carol City. Literally it was really small. He had a queen size bed with a black and red comforter set. He had a futon in the corner and a kitchen that didn't hold a stove. It was a fridge, a sink and a little counter space for a microwave and a toaster... other than that he had a hot plate... I guess that he can use if he wanted to cook something. A big flat screen was mounted on the wall in front of his bed but instead of having a dresser, he had clothes bins filled with clothes and clothes overflowing the closet. On the other free wall there were unlimited shoeboxes with every different style of shoe from Jordan, Nike, ferragamo, Burberry, Gucci, and everything else. He had a very small restroom but other than that this was it.

I plopped down on the bed waiting for his response. "Do it look like I could possibly live in this small ass box with anybody else?" He chuckled removing his watch from his wrist sitting it on the kitchen counter. He removed his gun from the small of his waist and then put one on the top of the closet and the other under the bed mattress.

"You live alone?"

He nod his head, "yep... been here for a year now but it's cool though. A nigga bout to be 18 in a few months."

Damn, that was tough. "Where your parents?"

He took a seat next to me removing his bloody Armani Exchange shirt from his body exposing his black wife beater and toned muscles. Pete had tattoos all over the place. I guess since I'd never paid him much attention, I hadn't even noticed that. "Never knew my daddy and my ole bird is still around, we just don't get along like that so I make my money and do my own thing."

"Hustling right?" I asked using my finger to interlock and twirl within' his. He allowed me to.

"Whatever it takes." He told me.

"So if you got money to take care of yourself then why you still in school and everything?"

"Bari... that don't got nothing to do with nothing. I hustle but I aint no dummy. That don't mean I wanna be doing this shit the rest of my life."

Oh Lord... he was making me actually like him and this wasn't a part of the plan. Like Tuff was my man, my main man and I wasn't leaving him.... I don't think there was nobody that could make me leave Tuff. Bambi seemed to think that he manipulated me cause I was so young but in reality, she just really didn't understand our bond. She hated Tuff and I know there was nothing more she would want than to see me with somebody else and Pete was a good candidate.

"I hear you Pete... I can only respect that. How's your head?" I asked.

"It ain't nothin' I'm aiight."

I removed my hand from his and used them to unbuckle his belt. He stopped me. "What'chu doin' Bari?" He looked deep in my eyes.

I felt bad in the pit of my stomach. The only dick I'd ever let feel me was Tuff's and I wanted to cry knowing I was about to cheat on him but I had to do what I had to do. "Shhhh." I said in a whisper. "Just let me take care of you." I told him ready to give him some of the best sex he ever had in his life.

~~~~~~

Three hours later, it was one something in the morning and we were back in front of my building. Sex with Pete was something I couldn't describe with words beyond amazing. Everything about it was different. The way he touched me, the way he kissed me, the way he asked me if I was okay multiple times during the sex. His dick was bigger, he was more passionate, and he aimed to please me. I honestly didn't think it could get any better than Tuff but now I was seeing much different. I understood why Tuff tried to keep me away from the young boys... he knew what would happen if I got a taste of them but now that I'd crossed that line with Pete... I wasn't so sure I could stop.

"You okay?" He asked me again as we sat there.

I nod my head, "yes."

"Well then why you look like you about to cry?" He asked me forcing me to look at him. I'm not gonna lie, I felt bad for what I was about to do to him. In exactly six weeks I'd be calling him telling him I'm pregnant and the baby is his.

"You'd never understand Pete." I sniffed.

"Try me." He replied.

I managed to force a smile. "Maybe another day, but right now... I gotta get inside before Messiah starts putting an APB out on me." I reached over and kissed his cheek. "Call me tomorrow."

"Wouldn't have it no other way." He said getting out and walking around to open the door for me and let me out.

"Awww such a gentlemen." I chuckled.

"Whatever yo." He smiled at me showing those gold teeth I loved.

I stepped out and walked toward the steps of my building while waving at him.

"And Bari!" he called out to me.

I turned around, "What's up?"

"Just know you mine now..." he told me without even shying away from me.

I swallowed hard wondering what the hell I'd just gotten myself into, but all I could do is smile and agree with him. I held my hand up to my ear again intimating a phone reminding him to call me, and then I raced upstairs so I could shower and go to bed. Sticking the key in the lock, it was dark as hell when I walked in but as soon as the smell of a cigar hit my nostrils, I knew that Tuff was in the apartment and sure enough, there he was sitting on the couch looking sexy as fuck with the little light from the TV bouncing off of his smooth face and perfect baby haired beard. I felt my heart rate pick up a little bit but I remained calm although I knew he was mad.

"Where you been?" he asked angrily. "You know what time it is?" he looked at his watch before blowing a cloud of smoke. Now if Sue wasn't here it was about to be a problem, but if she was here then I was safe cause although she loved the help Tuff provided when it came to her kids, she hated for the nigga to question us like we actually were his. Every time he would question me and Sue was around.... She thought it was because he was concerned but in reality he was questioning me out of jealousy cause I was his other woman.

"What I tell you about questioning my kids?" Sue walked from the back looking beautiful as ever... I had to admit that. Guess they were going out cause they both were all dressed up... this was the shit I was talking about right here. "You have fun Bari?"

"Yes..." I mumbled and faked a yawn. "I'm tired, I'm going to bed." I eased pass them both but I could still feel Tuff's eyes glued to me. He was pissed, I felt the anger bouncing off of him as if he knew I was up to no damn good. I wished he would once take into consideration how I felt every time I had to see him and Sue together. Like I loved my mama but I just wished she would leave my man the fuck alone. I made my way to my room and grabbed everything I needed for the shower so I could rinse the sex off of me, when I was done it looked like Sue and Tuff were long gone... Good!

I thought I'd feel better when I got in the bed but I was still heated so I pulled out my phone and sent Tuff a nice text message although he always told me not to do that, I didn't give a fuck.

To My world: I'm getting so sick of this shit. You keep telling me lies telling me you're gonna leave Sue alone so we can be together when it's time but yet you've been around the house more and more lately. What's going on Tuff? I can't even stop the tears from falling because this hurts me so bad. Why can't you see how much I love you? Is it too hard to love me back without loving Sue too?

I hit the send button and waited for a reply. It only took a few seconds for him to text me back.

From My world: Go to sleep... I love you.

I wanted to fucking scream... literally. Instead, I took my ass to sleep while feeling my heart breaking with every breath I was taking.

The next morning when I woke up, Sue and Tuff still weren't back, which was an indication they must've gotten a room somewhere or stayed at his house. I picked up the phone can called her. "Hey Sue... I was just calling to check on you." I said while scrambling me up some cheese eggs that I could slap on a piece of bread.

"Hey Belcalis... I was waiting for you to wake up... you wont believe I'm in Vegas!" She squealed.

"What?!" I blurted, "with who?"

"With Tuff! Who else?" She laughed. "He surprised me but I'll be back tomorrow night before you go to school Monday morning. Becka gonna come check on you and granna cooking Sunday dinner tomorrow so go eat over there..." she gave me a bunch of orders before hanging up. "Okay... love you... bye baby."

I didn't even have an appetite anymore, I ran to the bathroom instead standing over the toilet vomiting everything up. This whole situation was making me sick. He took good care of me as far as giving and buying me stuff but to take Sue to Vegas was just going over and beyond... meanwhile, I was over here being his best-kept secret. I washed my mouth out with tears running down my face and drag myself back to the kitchen where I then scraped the eggs from the pan and put them in the garbage. I took the bread and tied a knot in it throwing it back on top of the refrigerator. I checked the time on the stove; it was a little after 9:30 a.m. and my phone was ringing again.

"Messiah! Oh my God I'm so sorry... I'm heading across there right now." I tried to get myself together while talking to him since I didn't want him to know that I'd been crying. I had completely forgotten that I was suppose to watch Winter for Messiah today. "I'm coming, I promise."

"Come on Bari... I been waitin' on you for a hour but I bet you want some money though." He chuckled yawning.

"Lies!" I cracked a smile. "You act like I don't know you... you're still in the bed." I managed to smile... promise I'm coming now... my line beeping, gotta go." I said hanging up.

"Hello?" I answered.

"Morning Bacardi..." the deep voice said trying to be funny, clearly he knew Bacardi wasn't my fucking name.

I frowned, "who is this?"

"You don't know yo man voice?" he asked.

"Pete?" I laughed catching on to his voice.

He chuckled, "morning beautiful."

"Good morning to you too..."

"What'chu doin'?" he asked.

"Heading out to go babysit my niece... I call you as soon as I get settled. Promise."

"Okay... cool... do ya thang." He told me before hanging up.

I raced to the bathroom, brushed my teeth, threw on a pair of shorts with a crop top and then wrapped a lumberjack around my waist. I used a little water from the sink to brush my hair up in a ponytail and then locked up and raced across the way to Messiah's door using the spare key he gave me to open the door. I walked in with my hands covering my face. "Is it safe?!" I would hate to see you walking around naked." I joked.

"Auntie Bariiiii." Winter squealed jumping in my arms wearing her princess pajama set with her two wop-sided pigtails... I knew right then that Messiah had attempted to do her hair, I loved when he tried to at least comb it but I was gonna have to get my little niece right.

I kissed her cheek and gave her a tight hug. "I missed you sooo much." I kissed her over and over while she giggled away. Every time I saw Winter, she brought me some kind of peace, but looking at her today had me thinking about my own developing baby in my stomach.

"I missed you too." She said wiggling from my arms and then latching on to my hand. "Want to see all the toys daddy got me? Come..." she pulled me in her room, which looked much like a mini version of Toys-R-Us.

"Oh my gosh Winter." I laughed. "You're gonna get lost for sure in here with all these toys."

"And if my baby get lost you better find her or you gon' deal with me." Messiah said from behind me all dressed and ready to go. My brother was so fucking fine I was surprised he only had one baby mother around here. His dreads were neatly twist from the roots and I could tell he'd recently had a fresh wash and re-twist. Those thick brows were screaming at me and his beard was on point as usual. Today he wore a pair of Robin jeans with the brim of his Tommy Hilfiger boxers showing. A white wife beater graced his upper body freely showing his six-pack through the thin cloth along with his tattooed arms and neck, on his feet her wore a pair of Balenciaga sneakers. His iced out jewelry was around his neck and so was his Rolex that he never ever wore.

"My brother so handsomeeeee." I smiled. "What kind of cologne is that? Is smells decent as hell."

"Why? So you can try to go buy it for one of those little peanut head dudes you probably be tryna sneak around with? Got me messed up." He replied focusing on Winter. "Come give me a hug, daddy gotta go handle some business okay?" he kneeled down and received her in his arms as she hugged him. "Be good for Auntie Bari okay?"

She nod her head, "okay daddy..." she took off running back to her toys.

He stood up looking at me, "Heard you was at the party that got shot up last night... ion know when you gon' learn that sneaky shit ain't gon' get you nowhere. I can't protect nobody who don't wanna listen."

I don't even know why I expected him to not find out about that but I should've known better. "Trust me, after last night it wont ever happen again... that's my word."

"Heard the lil nigga Pete from around the way helped you."

"You know him?" I asked shocked.

He shook his head, "nope not personally but I heard a lot of good stuff bout lil dude."

I exhaled when he said that, now I didn't have to worry about him killing the boy. Distracting him from that conversation, I moved on to the next. "So where you in a rush to?"

"See a party planner..." he told me.

I furrowed my brows, hell, nobody in our family had a birthday coming up that I knew of. "For who?"

"For my lil mama... Qui." He replied with a certain look in his eyes. A look I'd NEVER seen before.

"Who the hell is that?" I questioned.

"Dad-ddy have a girlfra—ann." Winter giggled still playing with her toys, we didn't even think she was paying us any attention so we decided to move out into the hallway.

"You have a girlfriend?" I asked.

"You'll meet her at her party... you can come." He informed me.

The fact that he was inviting me out to a party around a bunch of other adults that weren't family was definitely progress. "I can't waittttt.... And omggggg you like her." I cheesed.

"You know you a real bug sometime Bari...." He looked at his watch.

"That's what little sister's are for."

He chuckled... "yeah, aiight I'll be back." He grabbed his keys and headed out the front door. When he was gone, I decided to go and call Pete back while playing with Winter... hell, wasn't shit else to do anyway since the love of my life was somewhere in Vegas showing Sue a good time while I was stuck to deal with teen pregnancy.... Sometime life really fucking sucked.

Chapter 8

Turquoise (Qui) Edwards

"Gu... it's wayyy too late and I'm super tired." I complained cause I really was. After he took his daughter to her mother, the first thing he did was pick me up from work and then kidnapped me for the day doing all kind of running around. I was kind of disappointed that I didn't get to meet Winter but I completely understood when he said he wasn't ready to bring any females around his baby girl until he was absolutely sure that they were worthy enough to even be around her. Honestly, if I had a child, I would've been the same exact way about he or she so for the most part, I stayed away when he was with Winter and saw him on his own time but it wasn't a day that went by that we didn't see each other.

Anyway, after he picked me up from work I already had a feeling he was up to something because he even had me get fitted for a special dress. The only thing I could think of was that he was trying to surprise me or something ever since Hulk mentioned my birthday coming up but he really gave himself away when he ask me for Hulk's number, which was strange to me... and then Hulk pissed me the fuck off because when I asked him about it he acted as if he didn't have a clue to what I was talking about as if he'd never spoke to Gu at all.

Now I was at Gu's house laid out on the couch still in my work clothes. I was trying to go home but he refused to let me go. I needed to take a damn shower and wash my long hair since I'd taken my faux locks out. "Gu pleaseee?" I begged with a puppy-dog face.

He flopped down on the couch with me and squeeze his body on the side of mine. Nuzzling his mouth against my ear he began to sing. "I know you wanna leave me.... But I refuseeee to let you gooo. If I have to beg and plead for your sympathy, I don't mind cause you mean that much to me... ain't to proud to beggg.... Sweat darlin'... please don't leave me girl." He playfully snapped his finger and mocked 'The Temptations'. Man that was one of my favorite movies. Messiah had me laughing so hard, I had to grab my stomach. Day by day I was falling in-love with this man. Every second, every hour on the hour. It didn't matter that I'd heard how dangerous he could really be... the side of him that I was getting, I could tell he didn't openly express too often so I had to take advantage of this. They say that love didn't come with a time stamped on it and I believed it because I was undeniably surrendering.

I muffled my laughter. "Gu stop.... You're embarrassing me."

That only made him grab me tighter as he carried on still singing, "Now I've gotta love so deep in the pit of my heart, and each day it grows more and more. I'm not ashamed to come and plead to you baby, if pleadin' keeps you from walkin' out that door."

"Okay Messiah..." I giggled with butterflies in my stomach.

"Yo you sure? Cause I'll get up and two step in this bitch." He said seriously.

"Oh hell no!" I laughed even harder shaking my head. "You good baby."

Aiight.. then, act right lil mama cause I ain't too proud to beg baby." He kissed me on my cheek.

"I thought you didn't beg though?" I challenged him.

"Been told you that you was worth that... stop playin' wit' me."

I never thought in a million years I'd stumble upon a man who kind of saved my life so he could kidnap me and was ready to probably kill me... and then fall for him. Since Messiah had been in my life, my days were brighter, my mind was at ease because as he promised... he would be here to make everything better wherever he could and so far he'd been true to his word. I found myself not even focusing on battling with my memory lost as much as I use to because Messiah gave me so much hope for the future, that I rarely thought about the past... and I hadn't even given up the panties.

"I smell like pizza... can I at least go home and shower?" I ask.

"Well I guess you my little pizza then." He said getting up off the couch. "Nah, I'll give you some boxers and a shirt and you can shower here. On the real, tomorrow is yo birthday and I got shit setup for you to get pampered all morning until I take you out... can a nigga at least get that?" H asked looking good enough to eat.

I had never spent the night at his place before, or no man's place for that matter so I felt nervous all-of-a-sudden and I guess the hesitation showed.

"What's that look?" He questioned.

"It's nothing." I shrugged standing up.

He gently wrapped his arm around the small of my back and pulled me close, "what I tell you about that? Tell me."

My eyes bounced around his living room as I cleared my throat. "I've never spent the night with a man before..."

He cut me off, "and nothing ain't gon' happen that you don't want to happen, that's my word... like I told you before, it's when you ready. I'm not pressin' for no pussy lil mama... I've been gettin' it for a long time now..."

I always respected his honesty but that didn't mean that it didn't make me feel some kind of way. Like whatever I would ask him, he would answer with no problem and always kept it real, but the more I was falling for him, the more difficult it was becoming to deal with his truth... then again, I'd probably run if he was full of lies. I knew when I met him he had some hoes but I can honestly say that since we'd been kicking it that shit died down a lot, and I had to respect that. Now, I wont lie and say I didn't feel a little insecure sometime cause while I was good looking, I didn't have shit to offer Gu... nothing at all and I'm sure that a nigga like him had to have ran across some bad bitches in his twenty-two years. Gu was so fine I was sure he could even get any chick he wanted to take care of him 'IF' he was really that kind of nigga.

"Why me Gu?" I involuntarily blurted out what I was thinking.

I could tell that caught him off guard, "what you mean?"

"I have nothing... nothing at all to offer you. I'm a student with a little part-time pizza job... I'm barely getting by Gu... you can have anybody you want and I'm sure of that."

For the first time, Gu actually lovingly looked me in my eyes. "Let me tell you somethin' lil mama... a job is a job... a check is a check... oatmeal is better than no meal so stop lettin' your doubts define yo hustle. You got it in you to do better and that's what you settin' yo'self up for... that's the kind of shit I like. You ain't comfortable bein' in the position you in. Its bein' uncomfortable that's gon' force you to be a go-getter. Now if you wasn't tryna do that then we'd have a problem. You a queen in my eyes and I'ma tell you that shit everyday till you finally get it."

My lips trembled as I tried to fight back the tears, "Awww Gu." A tear dropped.

"Yo cry baby ass." He teased now wrapping both his arms around me. I hugged him back placing my head on his chest in the process while taking in the scent of his YSL cologne. "I tell you what... I'ma take the couch and you take my bed. Go to sleep and I'ma wake you up early in the morning."

"Okay... that'll work." I agreed.

He grabbed my hand before I walked away to go shower. "And lil mama... don't think I'm gamin' you cause I'm not. Honestly, the way I feel about you is some shit I don't think I've ever really felt, even with my baby mother and I've done a lot of shit for her... even loved her at one point. But this bond we're buildin'.... This homie, lover, friend shit is somethin' I've never done. And for the record... you do more for me even when you think you don't, and it don't got shit to do with yo pockets ma."

"What you mean?" I asked trying to make logic of what he was saying.

"You work, go to school, and still manage to go home and cook just to make sure I get a hot meal, when Winter was here... you showed up outside my door with plates for us both and didn't even feel no type of way about me not wanting you to come inside and meet her, most females would've flipped the fuck out. When I'm havin' a bad day...

yo smile brighten that shit right up. When I forget about certain shit I gotta do, you come thru like my personal assistant makin' sure I don't miss shit. When I needed to flee my baby mother crib that night... you was my get away driver." He said winking at me. I had to hold in my laughter thinking about that night and till this day he still refuses to tell me what he did. I remember I was so mad at him that he didn't tell me that was his baby mother's house till after the fact. I remember wanting to even kick her ass when I saw all the little scratches on his face like she was trying to dig his skin out or something. "All in all... a female is suppose to make a nigga life easier, not harder, and you givin' me some kind of piece in my life is worth more than any dollar can add up to... aiight?"

With a smile, I wrapped my arms around him and gently kissed his lips before pulling back. "I really appreciate you."

"Same here lil mama... Go ahead and do what you gotta do so we can get up early. I got a whole day planned for you. It's fucked up that you feel like you ain't never had shit special done for you on yo birthday's but I'ma change all that."

I swallowed the lump in my throat no longer trying to mask my happiness because happiness is what was bringing the life back out of me. "I guess I'll see you in the morning love." I smiled walking off to go and shower. When I finally made it to Gu's bed, I think I must've fell asleep as soon as my head touched the pillow but by 8:00 a.m. Gu was fully dressed standing over me waking me up.

I immediately tossed the covers back over my head. "It's too early." I groaned.

"Happy birthday to youuuu, happy birthday to youuu. Wake up lil mama, I got you somethin'." He pulled the covers back off. The smell of food tickled my nose.

"What is it?" I ask finally sitting up covering my mouth trying to mask my morning breath. Gu stood there holding a tray of food and I couldn't help but to giggle. On the tray was a waffle, pan sausage, cheese eggs, grits, toast, and a cup of orange juice. All the same exact things that I ordered on our first unofficial date to the Waffle House, only difference was it was home cooked. There were dozens of pink and red roses on the dresser with two huge number balloons floating with my age '20'. At the edge of the bed were a shit load of gifts. There were bags from Victoria Secret, Mac, the 'Pink' store, Neiman Marcus, Charlotte Rousse and Pandora. I swear on everything I loved I sat there and cried like a baby. I didn't ever remember feeling this special... EVER! And the fact that Gu went all out for me really pulled on my heart.

"Ma, you gon' grab the tray for me so I can stop standing here lookin' like a bellboy?" he asked chuckling while sitting the tray next to me on the bed. I giggled through my tears and propped myself on my knees to reach his height so I could wrap my arms around him and hug him.

"Gu... I don't even know what's in those bags... but thank you soooo much, for everything."

He wrapped his arms around me giving me the best birthday hug ever while nuzzling into my neck. "Ain't no problem baby, I told you I got you. Happy birthday lil mama."

"Thanks again." I pulled back from him with my mouth-watering ready to tear the food down. "Did you cook all this yourself?" I asked him.

"Hell yeah... a nigga can throw down too." He said all cocky like.

"Whatever." I laughed picking up the fork.

"I'ma be right back... you can just get yo'self together when you done."

"I don't have anything to wear and I'm NOT putting my work uniform back on."

"Got it covered," he threw his head up toward the bag from the 'Pink' store.

Putting two and two together, I nod my head.

After I ate and went through my many of gifts on the bed, I dressed in a simple sweat-suit outfit from the 'Pink' store and slid on my UGG's. When I came out, Gu was already outside on the stoop talking to a group of niggas. When he saw me, all conversation was ceased. "You ready?" he asked me.

"Yes, I'm ready." I smiled. It was mad early but it wasn't unusual to see a bunch of niggas already out hustling.

Gu walked back to the door to lock up and then we both got in the car. My phone was blowing up with Facebook notifications but all I cared about was the man who I was in the presence of. I relaxed and decided not to ask him any questions about where he was taking me and instead listened to him rap along with the lyrics to Money Man 'Boss Up' lyrics.

"I had to boss up for a check, I had to step on these nigga neck, I had to go and get a couple stripes, I had to trap all day and night, I remember those cold nights, I hit it just like I got out the pen, I bought a brick and I go get it in, I'ma boss I can override ya, com'ere girl let me get inside ya, com'ere girl let me jump behind ya, play with me I'ma come and find ya, I had to go get a couple stripes, I had to trap all day and night, I had to boss up for a check, I had to step on these nigga neck."

I felt like the luckiest girl in the world watching him take the last puff on his joint with those sexy ass lips. He bobbed his head riding through the streets like he owned them. The first stop was to a hair and nail bar. Gu walked me in and as soon as we got inside everyone stopped what they were doing to pamper me. I felt like such a princess. "You're leaving me?" I ask him noticing that he was ready to head out after he got me setup and comfortable.

He nod his head and bent down kissing me. "Yeah, gotta make some runs but I'll be back though. Let them do they number on ya lil mama. They already know how to do yo hair and everything."

"Well damn..." I smiled, not only was my nigga a boss, he didn't mind taking charge and now that he introduced me to real, I'd probably always hate lames and any nigga that came after him 'IF' there were gonna be any, would have to match his level or beyond. He was setting the expectations so high that I don't even think I'd ever look at another man. "Okay... see you later."

By the time I was finished getting my hair washed and styled, and then getting my nails and toes done along with a full face of flawless makeup... I wanted to cry once I saw myself. I tried hard to remember the last time I'd felt this beautiful. Getting all of the services really took the majority of the day but it was worth it. Just as promised, when I came out, Gu was just pulling up and ready for me. After I thanked each and every woman inside the salon that had anything to do with making me feel as beautiful as I did... we left.

Gu looked a little pampered himself when I looked at him. His tapeline on his hair and beard was fresh and his dreads were re-twisted from the root. While I was all into his looks, he wasn't worried about himself... he was too busy complimenting me. "Damn lil mama... you look beautiful." He told me grabbing my hand with his free hand and using the other one to steer the wheel. "No bullshit... I love it."

"Thank you." I cooed pulling the mirror down taking a look at myself again. My hair was styled with a full body wave sew-in with a part on the side. The stylist chopped and feathered it to the God's and my face was beat to death. This was the first time that I'd ever work professional makeup... well makeup period... even the 'Goddess Lashes' were beautiful and went perfect with the face beat. "You look handsome yourself..." I gushed. "I don't know where we going tonight but if it's anywhere where some hoes is at they're gonna hate the shit outta us cause babyyyy we look good."

"Man fuck them hoes bae..." He chuckled.

I looked down at my phone low-key feeling some kind of way that I didn't get not one birthday call from my family but it was all-good. I wasn't even gonna focus on that. Gu looked down at his watch and then at me. "We got an hour to get dressed before we have to be where we goin'."

"Where is that?" I finally asked. "And what am I wearing?"

"Don't worry about where it's at... and I picked up the dress you got fitted for yesterday. It's in the trunk."

"Okay." I decided to chill and ignore the butterflies in my stomach wondering what Gu had up under his sleeve. He wouldn't even stay in the room with me while I got dressed. Now although I got fitted for the dress, I never knew what it looked like but much to my surprise it was a bad ass black laced dress designed my Tom Ford. The shit fit me so perfect that I was almost convinced that the designer himself styled it for me. It was short with lace running down the sides and a little around the breast area with a little diamond cut opening around the stomach area. What stood out the most were the shimmering Swarovski crystals splattered throughout the dress. A pair of badass Giuseppe Zanotti heels graced my pretty feet and I didn't wear any jewelry cause I didn't need to... only a simple pair of diamond cut studs in my ear, which was also one of my gifts earlier. Looking myself over in the mirror one more time, I smiled and promised I wouldn't shed not one tear and ruin my makeup. I honestly would've stood there much longer if Gu wasn't at the door rushing me.

"Lil mama... what happen? You got in there and redesigned the whole damn dress? We gotta go ma!"

I rolled my eyes while laughing cause he always had some slick shit to say. I grabbed my clutch and opened the door. Needless to say when we both got a glimpse of each other, neither one of us could stop smiling. We looked like the King and Queen of the hood. Gu had on a badass black suit that I assumed was designed by Tom Ford as well.... And he smelled good enough to lick all damn night. I don't even think words could express what either one of us was thinking. He grabbed my hand and led me out the door like a true gentlemen. When we got downstairs I didn't see the Camaro anywhere, instead we were greeted with a badass black and Chrome Wraith in front of us. "Now look," Gu started. "Don't get all excited cause this 'Is Not' my shit... I only rented it for the night so enjoy this bitch while you can ma... cause tomorrow this pretty muhfucka goin' right back." He told me in all seriousness trying to mask his own smile.

"I don't care if it's only for an hour." I laughed. "I'm gonna enjoy."

Gu helped me inside of the passenger side and then went over to the driver side and got in to pull off. "You heard from your folks today?" he asked me when we pulled off.

"No." I shook my head, "they probably forgot but it's okay." He simply nod his head and kept driving. It took us thirty minutes to get to our next destination, which was 'Rooftop E11even' ... so many cars were around and the building itself was nice. As we pulled up to valet... I spotted my mother's car sitting to the side as if it was waiting to be parked. "My mama is here?" I ask with a look of confusion.

"Yeah, she's meeting us for dinner." He replied without giving too much emphasis on it.

Gu led me through the building, which had restaurants, but he confused me when he hopped on the elevator instead and then led us all the way to the top. By the time we got off we were on the rooftop, which also has a closed in club as well. "It's beautiful up here Gu."

"Come on." He led me inside.

"Surpriseeeeee!" Everyone yelled as soon as we walked in shocking the shit out of me, so much so that I almost took off running.

Gu caught me mid step, laughing "where you goin'?"

I turned back around and before in knew it, my eyes were filling up. "Wowwww."

"You bet not cry." He warned me with a snide smirk on his face, "I'm tellin' you... if you let a tear fall and fuck up yo mascara... ain't no way you standin' next to me lookin' like Dracula."

"Fuck you." I laugh playfully hitting his arm and then hugging him. "Thank you soooo much, for all of this. You really made my day and night. I'll never forget this Gu."

"You welcome lil mama... go ahead, go greet ya peoples." He told me as I scanned the crowd. I saw my parents, my grandmother, some of my cousins and even Rain was in the building. I saw a lot of faces from around 'Da Nolia' as well and everyone was dressed in all black. The building was nicely decorated and black and silver balloons were everywhere. On one side of the bar there was an ice sculpture with the numbers "20" engraved in it. The music was going and bottles were popping. I guess since I wasn't old enough to actually get in the club, Gu rented out the Rooftop where he could have his own rules and I could still enjoy myself. I briefly looked back at Gu to see him wrapped up in a conversation with two other dudes dressed just as fly as him wearing all black as well. He waved for me to come over to them. When I was right besides him he grab me around my waist and introduced me. "Bae, this my nigga Beans and Cortez... we more like brothers but you know how that shit go."

I extended my hand and shook both of theirs. Thinking how fine those niggas were too. A chick that looked much like the singer Ciara clung next to Beans and didn't bother acknowledging me so I ignored her ass too. "Nice to meet ya'll" I told Beans and Cortex both.

"Nice to meet you too." They told me after they shook my hand.

"Niggaaa... when the fuckin' weddin'?" The one named Cortez laughed. "This the first time you ever went out like this pimp... gotta admit, this shit real nice too."

Gu ignored the fuck outta him but I thought it was quite funny and I honestly loved to hear that kind of shit. The only thing bothering me was the chick he was with still grilling me. "You ain't gon' speak to my lady Monica?" Gu asked her.

"Hello..." she replied dryly speaking to me. She could've saved that shit.

Instead of shaking her hand, I gave a simple smile but I couldn't help but to notice the was the dude Cortez kept side-eyeing Beans and his girl Monica. Now I wasn't the smartest and I may have been a virgin but body language could tell a whole story and a play sometime and I was convinced that something was going on there but it was none of my business. "I'll be back baby... I have people still waiting for me to speak."

"I'll be back too..." the girl Monica said. "I need a drink." She walked right past me.

Making my way to my parents, who were fly as hell sitting at their reserved table with bottles in front of them, I could only smile happy to see them both... couldn't speak so much for Rain, who stood there looking at me crazy. I wanted to compliment her on her appearance cause she looked really nice but since she act like she didn't even wanna be around... I left it alone. "Hey mama, hey daddy..." I hugged them both.

"Babyyy you look so nice." My mama cooed hugging me. "It took everything in me to not tell you about this night."

"I thought you forgot about me." I admitted.

"Oh girl hush... not our baby girl... and that Gu is something else child. You better keep him." She winked at me.

"Let the girl breathe Benita... damn... can I hug my youngest daughter on her birthday." He pulled and took a puff from his cigar so he could hug me as well. "Happy birthday baby girl."

"Thanks daddy." I giggled giving him a really tight hug.

"You look nice...." Rain said to me dryly. "Happy birthday."

As bad as I knew she didn't want me to hug her, I did it anyway. "Thanks Rain."

She froze at first but then she forced herself to hug me back not wanting to alarm our parents. I felt the presence of a body directly behind me right before they wrapped their hands around my eyes. "Guess who dawlinggggg."

I spun around as quick as lightening. "OMGGGG Hulk???" I excitely wrapped my arms around him as he lift me from the ground hugging me.

"Happy birthday chica!" he squealed.

I was so happy to see him. "What are you doing here?"

He looked around like that was a no brainer.... "well who do you think put together all of this lovely décor for this fancy party of yours sissy pooh?"

Now it all made sense, "So you did talk to Gu then?" I giggled. "Sneaky, sneaky sneaky... but no seriously thank you so much!" I squealed. Hulk looked good in his all black as well.

"Hey, when the master calls with request for the princess... I come running... anything for my dawlingggg." He kissed my cheek pulling a small box from the top of his suit jacket and handed it to me. "Happy birthday."

"Thank you love." I cheesed while opening it up to see another pendant to add on to my Pandora bracelet that he purchased for me on my last birthday. "Let me introduce you to my family... Hulk, this is my mom Benita, my father Ricky, and my sister Loraine.... Everyone this is a good friend of mine named Hulk." Everyone spoke like they had some sense besides Rain, of course, she walked off. I don't know why my parents always acted like they weren't oblivious to her attitude toward me but it was really starting to get irritating. Like she only wanted to fuck with me when she wanted to fuck with me and it was getting on my nerves. Whenever she thought too much attention was being shown to me, she really acted super ugly.

"Make sure you see us for your gift before the night is over with okay?" My daddy told me. I nod my head in agreement.

"I'll be back Edwards... I need to make sure all the host are on top of everything or else master is going to be super pissed with me and I always deliver with nothing more than professionalism when I'm on a job.... drink up bitch." He winked at me and walked off leaving me laughing. It was crazy how I never noticed his flamboyant ways before, but then again... he was different in school and I guess I understood. Across the room, Gu was surrounded by a group of women but when he caught his eyes on him we were both drawn to each other like a magnet. I didn't care what nobody said... I think I was in love.

~~~~~~

Messiah (Gu) Carter

"My niggas stack they money just to spend it, cause when you die you cannot take it wit'chu, if you ain't beefin' bout the money what's the problem, don't worry bout my niggas cause I got'em."

Me and my niggas was havin' a good ass time as the sounds of Fetty Wap 'RGF Island' blast throughout the rooftop while the rest of the room rapped along and drank unlimited liquor. Only thing relatable about this song was it was the epitome of how me and my niggas lived this street shit.

"Now that Monica's ass ain't around we can have some fuckin' nigga talk." Beans clowned looking over his shoulder before turning back to me.

"Nigga why you act like it's a problem wit' Monica bein' around like she be buggin' you and shit...." Cortez chuckled. "Man ya'll niggas a trip."

Beans ignored him but he was a better man than me cause 'like brother's' or not... don't get outta line actin' like you tryna straighten me bout some shit that's technically mine.... Fuck outta here... but to each it's own.

"What ya'll think about Qui?" I asked' em both.

"Mannnn." Beans started, "I mean I knew you said shorty was bad but I didn't know she was that goddamn bad... you in trouble my nigga."

"Oh yeah?" I chuckled. "Please... share the fuckin' details."

"Yeah, cause I wanna hear this shit too." Cortez replied. "Take us to school then Beans."

He shook his head, "you niggas slow as fuck.... Gotta teach ya'll everything... but check it..." he started, we got ourselves prepared to have some good old fashion boy talk like we were on the basketball courts back in the day schooling each other on females. "Aiight, so it's like this, and no disrespect to you but Qui is bad... like bad-bad, which means that's hella problems. If yo girl bad as fuck, trust me, at least 3 niggas a day are tryna holla and take her from you. That's 21 niggas a week, 84 a month, and 1,008 a year. Nigga... ain't no bitch alive sayin' 'no' 1,008 fuckin' times!"

I was convinced! This nigga Beans ain't have a lick of fucking sense! But what he was saying probably had some type of truth to it and definitely something to think about. "Fuck that." I laughed hard as fuck for the first time all night. "Nigga you stupidddd yo! I'm 'dat nigga' and niggas need to know I'm pressin' bout my bitch... period, don't even look her way, she's off fuckin' limits."

"Foreal yo.... But you did spit some real shit." Cortez dabbed him up.

Beans was laughing him damn self but when we saw RaRa, Meka, Tricia, and the rest of their lil click walk in all conversation was ceased. "Awe shit." he said, "look like you bout to have a problem up in this bitch with RaRa slick talkin' ass poppin' up."

It didn't surprise me that they showed up cause it didn't take long for the word to get around 'Da No'... especially about a party. I don't think RaRa was dumb enough to come up in here and start some shit though.

"Want me to put the hoes out?" Cortez asked ready to take control as they head in the opposite direction... everyone except for RaRa, whom was heading our way.

"Nah... she ain't crazy enough to come up in here on no bullshit." I replied.

I smelled her sweet ass perfume before she was actually all up in our faces ignoring Beans and Cortez and only focusing on me. I knew she wouldn't speak to Beans anyway cause she couldn't stand his ass... not that he gave a fuck. Nigga couldn't lie, RaRa looked damn good tonight and even wore all black for the occasion. Her thick thighs were covered with long-shimmery black tights, and she wore a closed toe pump on her feet. Her black Chanel flair shirt was sequenced and she'd let her hair grow out a little and had it in a short cut style and curl. A nude colored gloss covered her lips and her eyeliner complimented her sparkling hazels. On top of that, it looked like she'd put on a couple of pounds but it looked good on her.

"Sup Gu?" She spoke proceeding to hug me but I wasn't even havin' that shit. Instead, I gave her my hand to shake it... she chuckled. "It ain't that serious, I come in peace." She said scanning the room.

"What'chu doin' here?" I asked.

"Humph... ain't no way I woulda missed this for nothing in the world Gu. I wouldn't believe it if I hadn't seen it myself. " she said sarcastically. "But I come in peace, just here to mingle a little and I'm out."

I didn't know what she was on but I thought I'd give her the warning now just incase she got some funny ideas... "Aiight, you wanna party... cool. But stay the fuck away from my shorty... I'm sure you don't wanna play with me."

"Don't flatter yo'self Gu... I'm not trippin' bout yo girl... trust me... she won't be around long."

"Nah, she will..." I replied really trying to hold my patience and not show my ass by chopping her in her fuckin' throat.

She smiled again, "Good to hear... and it was nice seeing you." She prepared to walk off.

"Yo, you want a drink or something?" Beans asked her tryna be funny knowing she'd say no.

She brushed him off, "nah... ion drink no more." And with that she was gone in the crowd.

"Man that bitch is the nuts." Beans clowned causing us all to share laughter.

"Aye look, ya'll make sure the place is secure for me while I introduce Qui to my people's." I asked my niggas knowing they didn't mind. When they walked away, I called Bari, Sue, Becka, and of course Bambi over to where I was cause you couldn't tell her she wasn't family. Hell, I even managed to get granna out the house and I needed to get this over with before she got irritated and bounced; granna couldn't stand bein' around too many people but since I was her favorite, she did anything for me. "I wanna formally introduce ya'll to my girl Qui." I told the women of my life.

"I saw her already." Bari squealed. "She's badddd too!"

"I never expected you to make the girl Turquoise your girlfriend nigga." Bambi playfully punched my arm. "That's a good look though."

"Well all praises to the most high." My granna squealed. Becka and Sue got their good looks from granna and their feistiness too. Granna was on the short side but she looked damn good to be in her sixties and moved around just as good as a 21 year old. "I hope this one is a nice decent girl."

"Come on, let's get this over with." Becka clapped her hands. "Got a sugar daddy over there in the corner waiting on me."

"Becka!" Granna squealed.

She laughed, "mama it's a joke."

Sue checked her watch, "come on call her on over here cause I have to leave in a few... I have to meet Tuff."

I nod my head and called Qui over. I could see the nervousness in her face but she relaxed as soon as she was in my presence. I made sure of that when I pulled in to me. "Baby... this my ole girl Sue, auntie Becka, Granna, my lil sis that you've heard so much about 'Bari', and her best friend Bambi."

"I remember Bambi from the day of the fish fry." Qui smiled extending her hand. "Nice to formally meet you." She told her.

"Same to you." Bambi smiled.

"Hey Qui..." Bari said next, "it's nice to finally meet you." Bari went in to hug Qui but my too my surprise, Qui froze like she saw a ghost... like Bari made her uncomfortable. I made a mental note of that shit, like she ain't have no reason to be intimidated by Bari, she wasn't the type of aggravating ass lil sister that wanted to start drama with my girlfriends.

Qui cleared her throat, barely smiling. "Um... nice to meet you."

Sue and Becka both hugged Qui at the same damn time catching her off guard but she had no problem embracing them back. "Girl you beautiful." Becka kissed her cheek. "Happy birthday."

"Thank you." Qui replied.

"Nice to finally meet you." Sue told her. "I'm sure my son had nothing but good things to say about me." She scolded me with a smile on her face. Who the hell was Sue and Becka tryna fool? They must've forgot that Qui was the same girl with me on the stoop that say they were tryna scam people outta they money during that fake ass fish fry, but whatever.

"Well, we save the best for last." Granna winked her eye at Qui. "Nice to meet you young lady... and thank you so much for making my grandson happy."

Qui politely smiled. "I hope I am." She rushed. "It really was nice meeting you all and thank you so much for coming..." she then looked to me. "Baby I have to go see my daddy before he leaves so he can give me whatever it was he wanted to give me okay?" She said kissing my cheek before running off. Shit was kinda suspect to me how she was all-of-a-sudden uncomfortable and ready to run off.

"Ya'll hungry?" I asked them.

Once they all told me they were, I walked them over to where the buffet of food was so they could help themselves. I prepared to walk away to go see what was up with Qui and her change in demeanor when I was distracted by a big commotion coming from the table Qui's parents were sitting at... *Awe shit.*

~~~~~~

Turquoise (Qui) Edwards

My night was going so good, I was the happiest girl alive but leave it to Rain to try and fuck everything up for me. She was really on her best behavior up until my daddy dropped the key to a brand Infinity Q50 in my hand.... She fucking lost it! I don't know if it was the liquor, or her true feelings but it was on and popping.

While everyone around me thought that was sweet of my parents to get me a brand new car, Rain diverted all the attention back to herself clapping extremely loud. "QUI-DOES-IT-AGAIN!" She laughed hysterically. "I wanna be just like you when I grow up!"

I tried to ignore her and let my parents handle the situation, "What's gotten into you Rain... stop all that fucking carrying on girl. I done told you about acting all crazy for no reason." Our daddy snapped trying to stay cool as well. Meanwhile, my mother sat back in her seat embarrassed beyond embarrassment and decided to stay out of it hoping that my daddy could handle it himself.

"Nah, fuck that! Ever since we were little everything was Qui this and Qui that... this lil bitch was spoiled rotten. Ya'll never wanted to do shit for me cause she was the prettiest, she was the smartest... she had the better body..."

I felt a stabbing in my heart when she said that but it seemed like now she was really displaying her true feelings really getting down to the bottom of what her real problem was with me. The stream of tears instantly ran down my face while staring at my big sister, whom I had so much love and respect for. "Rain... none of that is true." I said.

"Stop that crazy ass talk Rain, you know better than I do that you'll were treated equally. Hell, you want a car? Is this what this is all about? We'll get you a car too Rain." My dad tried to sympathize with his oldest daughter, whom simply wasn't trying to hear it.

"Fuck you Qui." She snapped ignoring my daddy. "How the fuck you know what's true and what's not true?" She taunted. "You don't even know shit about yo' muthafuckin' self bitch... you can't remember shit!"

I don't know what happened, I remembered everyone gasping, I remember Hulk trying to hold me back in my ear telling me to just be the bigger person but I couldn't. I'd always been the bigger person and I just simply couldn't do it no more. I was positive that I probably couldn't beat Rain in a showdown cause she was much thicker and solid than me but I no longer gave a fuck. I was tired of her disrespecting me. I passed my key to my brand new whip to Hulk, who was still on the side of me and then I took a swing connecting with the left side of Rain's face as we both went down to the floor wrestling each other. I mean shit was crazy as we literally went blow for blow. With both my hands wrapped around her neck, I think I tried to choke the life out of her. The only way we were pulled apart was when Gu lift me and my daddy grabbed her... but that didn't stop neither one of us from kicking a screaming.

"Come on bitch!" I yelled. "I'mma fuck you up you jealous ass hoe! I never did shit to you! Never!"

Gu had me in a bear hug trying to keep me calm. "Calm the fuck down lil mama." He growled in my ear. "You got the shit off ya chest... you got her... now chill."

"Fuck you bitch!" Rain yelled trying to get out of my daddy's grip. I could see the hurt in his eyes to see his only two children having it out like this in front of all these people.

"Loraine! Turquoise! Ya'll stop this shit right now!" My mama finally stepped up trying to control the situation. I wasn't done though, I wanted to get the rest of this pressure off my chest and I had lots of it.

"Nah fuck that! She been asking for this shit! You's a fucking hater but you gon' get these hands tonight bitch!" I spit across the room missing her by an inch causing it to hit the wall instead.

Before I knew it, a shoe was coming across my face. Rain moved so quickly I didn't even see it in her hand. The impact from the heel hit me so hard, I immediately dazed out feeling extra dizzy as Gu's arms tightened up around me. From his grip alone I could tell he was pissed but outta respect for my parents he didn't wanna say anything at all, everybody at the party was lost as fuck about this situation.

"Yeah! What now talking ass bitch!" My sister continued to taunt me but I couldn't even respond. My head was in excruciating pain and if it want for Gu... I probably would've just hit the floor. For a second I think I blacked out... it was like I knew everyone was around me, but I couldn't put hear anything they were saying, it all seemed muffled.

I did manage to hear my mother's voice, "What's wrong with her?"

If I didn't know any better I'd say she was crying.

"Lil Mama! Qui! Qui!" I heard Gu's voice as my mind drift away scaring the shit out of me as I had flashbacks from the past.

"Qui! I got my restricts now girl!" Rain squealed running inside of the house interrupting me from doing my homework. "And look..." she dangled keys in my face, "daddy said we can hold his car."

I was excited for Rain, but I was kind of scared to be around her alone since she always tried to beat me up whenever I didn't want to do what she said. Prime example. My fourteenth birthday, which was a couple of months ago she told our parents she wanted to take me out to the movies but we ended up at a hotel where she made me give oral sex to three boys so they can pay her for it. I sat at the kitchen table cringing even thinking about it. I begged her not to make me do that but she slapped the shit out of me for crying and being a pussy. She even pulled out a recorder and taped it threatening that if I didn't do what she wanted she'd spread rumors in school that I was a little hoe, or a young dick sucker. I had no idea what I was doing but if it was gonna make my sister love me instead of hating me, then I did it. She didn't even take up for me when I vomited all over one of the boy's penis and he cursed me out.

Now she wanted to me to go take a ride with her and I didn't trust her. I wanted to just be a good girl and finish my homework but she wanted to do other things. Rain never like me since I was born, she always felt as though I was the spoiled one, the goody two-shoe and everyone appraised me when in reality it wasn't that. I was just an respectful child and Rain was the one always in trouble because she was so rebellious. Whatever my parents told her to do, she always did the opposite. She was the type of big sister that popped all the doll heads off of my Barbie's and then let me find them floating in our bathroom toilet just so I could stick my little hands in the nasty water and dig them out. My parents had no idea how badly Rain mistreated me because whenever they were around.... Rain acted like the best big sister in the world. But she was really the big sister from hell. "I'm happy for you Rain." I smiled. "Was it hard?"

"Girl, hell fuck no..." she laughed. "I'm a pro at everything I do."

It was crazy to me how we could talk about anything when she was in a good mood and actually wanted to be nice to me, which wasn't often... but it was something totally different when she wanted to sabotage me. "I can't wait until it's time for me to get mine... daddy said he'll buy me a car if I can ace it on the first try." I told her immediately regretting my words before they even completely escaped my lips. I knew better than to ever mention anything that was being done for me because Rain was so competitive. Everything was my fault... she even hated me because at fourteen years of age, I was only focusing on school... but when she was fourteen she was getting caught sucking dick behind the portables at school and no matter what the girls or boys in our neighborhood said about my sister, I always took up for her. "I'm-I'm sorry Rain, I wasn't trying to be boastful." I apologized.

She smiled and pulled me out of the seat, "girl don't trip... it's all good I'm not trippin' hell if I get my act right I'm sure I'd get a car too... now let's go get something to eat cause daddy is out back mowing the lawn and mama is was getting late... you wanna eat right?" She asked with a smile. I guess I was kind of hungry since I hadn't eaten anything since lunch. Reluctantly I closed my notebooks and got up to leave with Rain. I hopped in the passenger seat and she hopped in the drivers seat.

"Shouldn't we wear seatbelts?" I suggested.

"Hell no." She chuckled trying to drive like she was cool as we drove on the back streets. "That's for the nerdy kids."

"Okay..." I shrugged. "Where are we getting food from?"

"Bojangles... I want some chicken and biscuits, "what about you?" She asked looking over at me noticing how tense I was. "Relax Qui... I've been stealing the car long before I got restricts... I can drive."

"I think it's pretty cool that you're driving." I smiled.

She looked over at me again, "you know, we've only got a few more miles before we get there and nobody will be on this back street... I can teach you how to drive if you want... that's if you aint scared." She teased. "Cause you know you a goody two-shoe.

"I'm not!"

"Yes you are!" She stuck out her tongue. I didn't like being looked down upon at all and I'd show her that I wasn't scared.

"Pull over! I'll try it."

She immediately pulled over and we switched spots. I went to put my seatbelt on and she stopped me. "Remember that's for the nerds... we the cool kids."

"Um-okay Rain but I don't know about this." I said nervously.

She sighed, "Qui, don't worry about it... I got you... promise. Now put your hands on the wheel and then ease off from the side, don't hit the gas hard."

I did as I was told and surprisingly it wasn't that bad, well... it was bad but not as bad as I thought it would be. "Go faster girl it's okay, you're only doing 20."

I hit the gas a little harder as my hands shook uncontrollably. "Rain I wanna slow down."

"Stop being a pussy, how you gonna become a pro if you scared... go faster."

I was up to 40, "Rain." I said with trembling lips, "this was a bad idea."

"GO A LITTLE FASTER QUI! YOU PISSING ME THE FUCK OFF ALWAYS ON THIS SCARY SHIT!" She yelled in my ear now putting her seatbelt on. I was up to 65 in a 35mph zone.

"Rain I'm scared!" I yelled when I felt the car swerving, I was losing control! "I have to stop!" I said noticing a huge light pole coming up and just thinking to myself that I was gonna end up hitting it if I didn't stop the car. "I'm stopping!"

We were only a couple of feet away from the pole when I felt Rain's hand on the back of my head, no you're not bitch! Whap! My head hit the steering wheel and the car went out of control hitting the pole. I heard the sounds from the impact of the crash, I heard sirens, I heard the dispatchers asking me my name and then everything was black.

I remember waking up in the hospital but I had no idea I'd been out for six whole months. When I finally did wake up, the only person by my beside was Rain for whatever odd reason but she looked like she was perfectly fine... why didn't anything happen to her? I remember thinking to myself. Had I had my memory, I would've surely remembered... the seatbelt... she put hers on at the last minute and didn't allow me to put mine on... when she rammed my head into the wheel she grabbed it and purposely ran us into that pole... my sister wanted me dead; ironically when I came to... I just simply couldn't remember.

"Qui! You okay baby?" Gu tried to snap me out of it. I don't know where the burst of energy came from but I was ready to kill that bitch of a sister!

"Where's Rain?!" I asked with tears falling down my wild ass, fuck the dress, fuck the mascara, Gu was gonna have to accept me being Dracula around this bitch. "Where is she?" I cried.

"Leave it alone baby, ya'll need to let this cool down." My daddy tried to help Gu console me as the onlookers looked at me with sympathy in their eyes. I cried so hard my body shook. "Pleaseee I have to talk to her." I begged looking in Gu's eyes. "Gu... I remember now." I told him. "Everything you and I talked about... I remember. Now where's Rain?"

Gu looked at me and automatically knew what I was talking about. "Mr. Edwards." He said respectfully to my daddy. "We gotta let her do this... she just found her peace, trust me."

Gu led me outside where Rain was standing in front of valet smoking cigarette. I hadn't expected the entire party to follow me outside but they did and I didn't care. I needed this, I had to confront my sister and I didn't care who was there to witness it. My parents were even outside now and while my daddy was pissed, my mother was hurt to see us like this. I was bare feet like a motherfucker since I had no clue what happened to my shoes but I didn't care. "Rain..." I said in almost a whisper.

She turned around looking at me without a remorseful bone I her body. "What?" She flicked her cigarette. "You wanna go for round two? And you brought the crowd to see you get your ass whooped?"

I shook my head trying to fight back the tears, "I remember everything now Rain." I trembled. "I remember.. the accident... everything. You did it... you tried to kill me."

With an evil smirk on her face, she didn't even try to deny it, "Bingo! You finally fucking remember!" She clapped her hands like she was applauding a show. "Bravo bitch!" she then frowned and spoke to me with so much hatred dripping from her words when she ask me. "Why the fuck couldn't you just die?"

"Man fuck that!" Gu snapped. "That's yo fuckin' sister yo." He grit his teeth.

"Fuck her." She hissed, "Bitch always thought it was about her! Tell everybody out here how you was a professional dick sucker before the accident. You gave three boys some dome at one time in a hotel room." She said in front of everybody.

"The fuck she talkin' about Qui?" Gu furrowed his brows in confusion.

"That's not gonna work Rain... you made me do that shit. You slapped me around and threatened to tell rumors about me. You made me do that for you... you fucking tricked me out for some money... your own sister. You can't humiliate me anymore Rain... this is my truth, my peace and I'm accepting it."

Now that she knew her humiliation wasn't working and actually backfiring, her eyes danced around the crowd of onlookers.

My mother was now in her face. "You did all that to my baby?" she asked Rain with a tear falling down her eyes. She was all choked up on tears.

"It's okay mama." I said trying to get her to walk away with me.

"I'm your daughter too..." Rain told her.

My mama shook her head, "I'm gonna ask you again... you did all that to my baby?!" She asked like a deranged woman.

This time my daddy tried to get her to calm down as her body visibly shook, "Benita, I'm mad too but let's just let this die down and talk about it tomorrow. It's apparent that we need some family counseling and a lot of help."

She snatched away from him still grilling Rain as she cried, "that's my fucking baby over there you little evil bitch! How dare you! How fucking dare you!"

Now Rain's tough ass was crying! "I'm your fucking daughter too! No matter how it happened and ya'll always loved her more!"

The fuck was she talking about no matter how it happened?

My daddy intervened again, "that's enough!" he was now choked up on tears. "This shit isn't for everybody! This shit aint no game show.... this is our life! And our family is in a crisis... we need prayer! Not a bunch of fucking bickering! Now Benita! Let's go!" He grabbed her by her arm and broke through the crowd to leave.

I gave Rain one last look, "You wanted me dead... well bitch I'll be dead foreal. I don't ever have shit to say to you... I'll let God deal with yo ass." I hissed.

Beans and Cortez were right by me and Gu's side, even the chick Monica who was now looking at me with tears in her eyes. Even Gu's family stood off to the side wiping tears. Hulk walked up to me and didn't even have any words with his red face flushed with tears... he simply hugged me really tight. "I love you chica." He told me before walking off.

My party was ruined, my night was ruined. Looking up in Gu's eyes, I saw nothing more than death. He was hurt for me and I could see it. "Baby, I'm ready to go home." I told him.

He nodded his head and gave the keys to my new car to Cortez. "Drive her car for me." He directed.

"Which one is it Gu? Its fifty million infinity's out here."

"Hit the alarm and find it... shit I don't know, just let me get her home aiight..." he told him and then lift me in his arms in a cradle position since I didn't have any shoes on. I lay my head on his chest and closed my eyes. I wished I could wake up and all this shit be a bad dream but I knew when I woke up in the morning, it was still gonna be the evil truths of my reality.

Chapter 9

Messiah (Gu) Carter

"Qui..." I called her name sticking my head in my room door trying to see if she was still sleeping. I knew she'd been up all night studying for midterms so if she was sleep it was cool... I just wanted to make sure she was good before I left the apartment. "Qui..." I called her name again but she was knocked out. I walked closer to the bed and pulled the cover over her sexy ass body since she wore nothing besides a lace thong and the matching bra. It was tough being around lil mama without physically touching her but I knew she was vulnerable right now and when I got the pussy, I wanted her to be in the right mind-frame. Although it had been a couple of weeks since everything went down... I just knew she wasn't ready so the most I could do was cuddle with her every night and remind her that a nigga was still here.

She never went back to the apartment she shared with Rain and she didn't wanna go to her parents house so I let her crash with me for a lil bit, which I was skeptical about at first but it was cool so far, and now I was tight cause last night she told me she received her letter for her own subsidized housing and her apartment would be ready in a few days, which was in the building over from mine. If I could've stayed in the crib with her today, I would've but I had moves to make, plus Hennessy kept calling me every hour on the hour.

"Yeah?" I answered walking down the steps as the bright as sun bounced off of my face. "I hope it's important the way you blowin' my shit up."

"Winter is sick." She said dryly. She still had an attitude about me killing TuTu and all that other shit but I didn't give a fuck... she better had constantly remembered that night before she every thought about pulling another dumb ass move cause then it was gon' be worse than before. I never thought the day would come where Hennessy and me would be at this point but she lost all respect from me when she tried to keep Hennessy away... I was gon' be the nigga to show her not to play wit' no real nigga.

"What's wrong with her?"

"A cold and a fever.... And it's bad." She said.

"Aiight... I'll be there." I told her making my way across the street to Sue's building where everybody was already up and about doin' there thing as usual. I expected that shit, but what I didn't expect was for Bari to be sittin' on the stoop with some cool ass lil nigga. Bari looked like she wanted to run, meanwhile I was peepin' how lil dude ain't even shy away from me. Instead, he stood up as soon as he was within' arms reach and dabbed me up.

"Wus up Gu? I'm Pete... wus good wit'cha." He spoke with a lot of confidence and cockiness and I liked that. I always told Bari don't get caught up with no busta ass niggas. So this was that lil nigga I'd been hearin' about? I thought to myself. Heard he was makin' a lil name for his himself in 'Da No' and niggas was already stampin' him as solidified but what made me have a different level of respect for the nigga was upon hearin' about the two different incidents where he had to look out for Bari. Just cause I hadn't mentioned the first incident to her didn't mean I didn't hear about it... that was Bari's slick ass always thinkin' I didn't know shit.

"Wus good my dude..." I greeted him back. "Been waitin' to see you so I can thank you for lookin' out for my lil sis and shit wit' that Dro situation and the other shit at the lil house party that night." I went in my pocket to pull out a couple of hundreds for his pockets just off GP of him lookin' out.

He stopped me, "Nah... ain't no problem. No disrespect to you or nothin' but I've been waitin' to see you too." Pete admitted.

"Oh gosh." Bari put her hand in her face. "Messiah... please first just promise me you wont kill him." She said to me.

Now she was gettin' me tight thinkin' all crazy and shit. "Kill him for what Bari... the fuck you talkin' about?"

Pete interrupted looking at her like she was crazy as he shook his head. "Girls do the most sometime man."

I half chuckled and stroked my goatee; I liked his style.

"Anyway... I just wanted you to know that I like Bari... I like Bari a lot and I'm not one of these crabby patty ass niggas out here. I may be young but a nigga get it off the muscle and take care of himself ya dig?"

I examined him expressionless, "Aiight, nigga can respect that, but you said all that to say what? Spit it out young nigga."

"I'm sayin' with yo approval, I want Bari to be my girl." He got it out and while if it were any other nigga, their fuckin' lips would be on the floor right now... I respected how he came at me like a man and looked me in the eyes the entire time he was talking to me. A part of me didn't know how I felt about this shit cause I knew what these niggas were all about eventually, and I wanted Bari to stay focused. I stood there for a few seconds taking it all in. I wasn't ready for Bari to grow up, but when I looked at her sitting on the stoop with most beautiful glow ever... I had to accept the fact that she really was growing up and it wasn't shit I could do about it. I wanted the Bari that wore the pigtails and overalls, the one who came in the room and squeezed in between me and Ronnie when she had nightmares, I missed the Bari who got on my last goddamn nerve doin' all the little aggravating shit little sister's did... but now, it was time for me to accept the woman she was growing in to.

Without another thought about it I told Pete straight up, "You have my blessin'."

Bari's head shot up! "What?!" she asked confused. "Messiah, you are not letting me have a boyfriend. I know you playing." She then looked to Pete, "Pete don't take him serious he's gonna shoot you."

"Bari!" I laughed. "Sit'cho ass down... if Pete know anything about me then he know I wont ever shoot a nigga behind his back and I don't ever play up in no niggas face either... this a man thing, stay outta this."

Pete extend his hand to mine, "respect."

I shook his hand then balled my fist and lightly hit my chest twice, "Respect young dude... take care of my sister." I told him ready to walk to my car now.

"But wait!" Bari rushed behind me. "Are we still goin' to granna's house tonight for dinner? She's got meat on the grill today."

"Yeah... I didn't forget." I told her. That was my granna's way of gettin' everybody together, plus it was gon' be a good way to get Qui outta that apartment besides work and school. Shit, lil mama wasn't pickin' up for nobody besides me and Hulk. She hadn't even spoke to her parents yet and damn sho didn't speak to Rain. The last thin I wanted her to do was get depressed cause she's secluding herself from the world and I knew she wouldn't say no to some good ass southern style food. He needed to eat anyway cause I didn't want no skinny ass beanpole of a girlfriend... that shit wasn't gon' work for me.

"Qui coming?" She asked.

"Yeah, I'mma get her out." I told her... hell, not even my own family had seen her since the party cause I was keepin' everybody away from my apartment right now, that girl just needed to breath for a lil bit. "I'm goin' to check on Winter... I'ma holla at ya'll."

"Tell my niece I said hi." Bari instructed me as she sat back on the stoop.

I made my way to Walgreens to purchase some medicine for Winter and since a nigga ain't really know what to grab... I picked up half the shit on the shelves... shit, somethin' had to work. I never paid much attention to the chiming sound that let people know when somebody was walking through the door, but today while giving the cashier the money I looked up just in time to see RaRa's ass getting ready to come in until she saw my face and did an about face and turned her ass around. Grabbing the bag, I walked out to go to the car since I was in Qui's Infinity and not my own.... Probably why the silly ass girl ain't know I was in here while she was tryna run and shit. Scanning the parking lot, she was long gone. *The fuck was that about?*

While at the light, I pulled out the phone to call her ass only to be greeted with an recording. *'The number you have reached is no longer in service'.*

I smirked, "guess the bitch changed her number." I said to myself brushing it off tossing the phone in the passenger seat. Nigga ain't know what kinda weirdo shit some of these females be on, but I was glad she was finally moving on. Hell, who knows... maybe it was a bit much for her to still have to look me in my face so she rather not be in my presence... I understood. Lighting me a joint, I continued on my route and turned the music up bobbing my head to YFN Lucci 'Heartless'...

"Lately I been chasin' paper, chasin' guap, yeah, yeah. Lately I been feelin' like fuck a hater, fuck a cop, yeah, yeah. I swear lately I been heartless, heartless, heartless. Ain't no pressure bout no beef we gon air shit out, I got yo bitch and she tellin' all your whereabouts"

I pulled up to Hennessy's house and hopped out with all the shit my baby girl needed. I couldn't lie, the fact that was actually knocking on the front door and not using my own key was a different feeling but ironically that shit felt like a weight lifted from my chest finally feeling like I wasn't obligated for once. Hennessy greeted me at the door wearing a short silk robe without a bra nowhere in sight cause her headlights greeted me before I even saw her face. "Hey Messiah." She spoke. "Come on, come in." She stepped to the side.

I walked in and was smacked in the face with the scent of breakfast. "Where Winter?" I asked her.

She pointed to the backroom, "she's in there watching cartoons."

I nod my head and walked to her room. Winter was there on top of her bed sitting Indian style so engrossed in the TV that she didn't even hear me come in. "Daddyyyy." She squealed when she finally did look up looking like she was happy to see me.

I flopped on the bed with her wrapping my arm around her. "What's wrong with daddy baby?" I placed my hand on her neck and forehead to see if she was warm. I mean, shit I guess she may have been a lil warm but I didn't see shit wrong for the most part. No runny nose, no sneezing no nothing. Winter didn't have none of the symptoms that Winter tried to make it seem like she had.... The way she was talking I thought baby girl was in bad condition trying to fight a flu or something.

"Nothing." She giggled. "Can I go with you?" She asked with pleading eyes.

I tried hard to disguise my anger in front of Winter but in the back of my mind I was low key pissed cause I see Winter was about to start playing these games again, she knew I had a bitch so I guess now she felt like it was time to see what kinda games she could play and she had me fucked up. "I'll see okay? Let me go talk to yo mama and I'll be back."

She nod her head, "Okay."

When I made my way to the kitchen, Hennessy had her back turned scrambling some eggs so I stood there leaned up against the counter with my arms crossed waiting for her to turn around.

"Shit!" she gasped when she finally did dropping the fork on the ground that was in her hand. When she bent down to get it... she gave me a full shot of ass and pussy since she didn't have panties on. "You scared the shit outta me." She frowned throwing the fork in the sink.

I knew right then what this was about, Hennessy was tryna get some dick and this was the shit I was talking about, this how we always got caught right back up in the cycle, but not this time... I wasn't lettin' the pussy get the best of me cause that shit came with too much bullshit behind it coming from Hennessy... nah I was good she could keep her lil pussy. I'd rather beat my meat first no matter how tempting fucking her was.... Especially since it was easy pussy.

With a straight face I asked her, "Yo, why you call me over here like my baby was sick as fuck? Man the girl in the perfectly fuckin' fine."

"Really?" She asked looking unbothered going back to doing what she was doing. "Humph, she must feel better then... thank god."

This bitch.... I said to myself shaking my head.

"Yo, find you another whack ass nigga to play with Nessy, cause a nigga like me don't got time... all the time on my hands is much needed... you done made a nigga go buy all this shit for what? To feel like you still got some kind of power, or to play games?"

Silence.

"Yeah, just like I thought... stop fuckin' playin' wit' a nigga, when I said that shit was done, I meant it." I turned to walk out.

She ran around me blocking me from leaving. "Messiah! Wait!"

I furrowed my brows, "what?" I looked down at her waiting for her to say what she had to say.

"Can we talk about all of this?" She asked using her hand to gently grab my arm.

I took a step back and shook my head, "hell nah we can't talk if it ain't about Winter... period."

"But why it gotta be like that? We better than this, we can at least be friends Messiah."

"Ain't this bout a bitch?" I chuckled. "No the fuck we can't... you made it like this when you showed me you could act like a bird bitch and try to take my daughter from me. The moment you did that, shit changed, my outlook on you changed. I never would've thought you would've did me like that so fuck it."

She sighed, and I could tell she felt like shit. "Messiah, I'm sorry."

"Yeah... me too." I stepped around her ass and headed to the door. "Yo, lock up and tell my baby I'ma call her later on."

I didn't even wait for a response, I left Hennessy in the house where she belonged and probably with a wet pussy. Fuck that... she should've never played with a nigga like me cause I wasn't the average baby daddy now I didn't even wanna have a friendship with her ass. Show me you don't give a fuck about me and I'ma fuck ya feelin's up three times harder.

I pushed the shit with Hennessy to the back of my mind and made some runs. My final run was by the grocery store to get some extra meat and shit for granna them to put on the grill since it was almost time to over there. When I got to the crib, I backed in and left the shit in the car since we were heading right back out anyway. Bambi was on my side of the building making her rounds hustlin' like she normally did.

"Sup Gu?" She spoke counting her money.

"Sup Bam... let a nigga support da hustle, what you got today?"

She looked in her bag, "I got one brownie, three cookies, a gummy bear pack and two rice Krispy treats... after that I'm sold out till tomorrow and you know I got the best weed treats in town so you better get it while you can."

I reached in my pocket and gave her a fifty. "Here, let a nigga get a cookie and a treat."

"Here." She gave it to me.

"Aiight... I'mma see you around later on... gotta go." I ran up the steps and used my key to walk in my apartment. The smell of Febreeze tickled my nose and everything was spotless, which was an indication that Qui had cleaned up. "Qui!" I called her name. she wasn't nowhere in the apartment and the bed was fully made up. I notice the key to my Camaro was gone so I called her.

"Hey love." She cooed.

Her voice was like music to a nigga ears, made my whole day. "Sup lil mama... you okay?" I asked her.

"Yeah... I met Hulk at Cold Stones for some ice cream since he was so determined to get me outta the apartment... plus you were taking too long to come back but I didn't wanna call you bothering you and shit."

That shit made me feel a type of way, "you can bother me... you can call me whenever you feel the urge too, unless you become a bug then a nigga gotta block yo ass."

She laughed, "whatever Gu."

"Well look, I came back to pick you up but since you gon' I'ma just text you granna address. She's cookin' dinner and everybody gotta be there, she specifically requested that you get out the house and have yo ass there... and trust me, you don't wanna piss granna off.... Not a good look ma."

"Well, since you put it that way, then I guess I don't have a choice although I'd prefer to stay inside and watch Netflix."

"Lil mama, I can't tell you how to feel but I can't let you do that to yo'self.... Not on my watch, you gone fuck around and be depressed." I shook my head and grabbed the keys to head back out. "Look, just meet me there aiight? I'm headed there now."

"Umm... okay Gu." She agreed, I still heard the hesitation in her voice but it brought some comfort knowing that she would be there. "It's just that..."

"What?"

She took a deep breath, "I haven't seen anyone since the party and Rain said all that nasty evil shit to me in front of everybody Gu... she even went as low as tryna make me look like a hoe and that was very degrading... and embarrassing and now you want me to go look people in the face? I just don't know if I'm ready."

That shit hurt me to even know that she was ashamed about some shit that wasn't her fault. I cant lie, it fucked me up as well to finally hear about her past. I wanted to knock Rain's muhfuckin' head off in that bitch, take that bitch right off the market... but outta respect for Ricky and Benita... I couldn't do it. I had to chill. I tried not to think about all the shit Rain said, and I wanted Qui to be able to get past it too. "Qui at the end of the day, anybody there with some common damn sense ain't lookin' at you crazy or judging you and if they are... trust they can deal wit me... period. Besides, my people ain't like that anyway... bein' from the hood ain't shit we ain't seen or heard aiight?"

"Okay... I hear you." She replied.

"You okay?"

"Gu you always make me better even when I don't think I can be."

She was the only person who could put a smile on my face as easily as she did, "Good, I'ma see you in a lil bit, and drive safe shorty."

"It's lil mama..." she corrected me.

I licked my lips and chuckled, "Aiight lil mama."

~~~~~~~

"Granna!" I called her name while I stood over the grill sweatin' flippin' meat and shit. "You told me to come eat, you ain't tell me I was the one cookin' the meal."

"Boy shut yo ass up." She laughed while sitting around all the other women of the family while they drank or chill with their feet in the pool.

"I'm just sayin'... hell I woulda wore my raggedy stuff. Now I'm messin' up my good shit... you know how much this shirt cost?" I pulled off Saint Laurent shirt and sat it to the side exposing my wife beater.

The music started playin' and none of them were payin' me no attention, meanwhile I was about to call Qui wondering where my baby was at or if she got lost... I kinda missed lil mama. Looking over my shoulder, I saw Bari sitting off to the side by herself all wrapped up in her phone. I don't know what was going on with her cause earlier she was the happiest girl in the world, glowing and shit, but now she was looking all pale like she didn't wanna be bothered. I was all prepared to call her over and see what was up with that shit but was distracted when Qui walked in looking good as fuck. Nigga dick instantly got happy just lookin' at shorty.

Qui often underestimated herself but she really was beautiful as fuck. She locked eyes with me and smiled before she went to greet everybody giving out hugs, but when it came to Bari... it was a simple wave. I couldn't figure that shit out for the life of me cause I always wanted the girl I'ma be with to have a good ass relationship with my sister but when it came to Bari... Qui was very standoffish and that shit blew me. I was gon' ask her about that shit when we got back to the crib. Maybe it was cause of how her relationship was with her own sister, that affected her from wanting to get to know my sister... and if that was the case, I understood but I still wanted to address it.

"Hey baby." She wrapped her arms around me from behind resting her head on my backside.

"Sup lil mama..." I flipped a piece of steak and then took a swig of my Heineken before turning around placing a wet kiss on her lips. "You aiight?"

"Yeah... I'm fine." She answered looking up at me with love in her eyes.

"Where ya bestie... Hulk?"

"Man problems." She giggled.

I shook my head, "please spare me the fuckin' details...." I chuckled and then told my family. "Aye! This shit bout ready! Ya'll can start fixin' plates... I'm bout to bring all the meet inside in a few!"

That was all I had to say and everybody was up and makin' they way inside of granna's house not wanting to miss out on none of the good food she had scattered in pans all across her dining room table, all they wee waiting for was the meat and that was ready so now it was time to dig in. My phone rung and since my hands were full, I told Qui to pull it out my pocket for me. "What it say?" I asked her.

"Tuff..." She replied.

I nod my head, "put it on speaker." I told her. "Yo Tuff!" I yelled in the phone. "The fuck you at mayne? You shoulda been here helpin' a nigga flip all this meat."

"Gotta get the money nigga... that shit that make the world go round." He laughed. "And I know damn well they aint have you on no grill... I know all that shit gotta be burned fo'sho."

"Man sheitttt... you better ask bout me. You may have taught me the grillin' game but I'm the one mastered that shit and took it right from you." I reminded his ass.

Tuff fell out laughin'. "Oh hell nah, lil nigga it's on now. I'ma buy me a brand new grill next week and show you the mastermind behind what these hands do."

"How much you puttin' in the pot then?" I challenged him.

"A dub..." He replied.

"A dub?" I asked still laughin'. "Nigga you must be crazy."

"Ya mama take all my money... shit the fuck you want me to do?"

"You gotta come better than that Tuff."

"Aiight a hunnid..."

"I can fuck wit' dat." I told him.

"Bet..." he agreed. "And I'm outside, tell somebody come let me in."

"Aiight..." I hung up. "Yo! Somebody let tuff in!" Nobody answered me since they were tryna cuff extra plates to take home and we hadn't even fixed real plates yet... just like black people... I shook my head.

Qui laughed at me, "I'll go open the door baby, don't worry about it."

"Thanks lil mama... don't go too far... nigga miss you."

"Never..." She winked at me.

It only took a couple of seconds before I was in the house sitting the meat down and everybody was mingling... once again except for Bari. "What up wit'chu?" I asked her.

She sat at the table with food in front of her but she wasn't touching none of it. "Nothing..." she mumbled.

"Yo, you on ya period or somethin' Bari? The way yo mood swings change is crazy. I don't understand women. Like you only sixteen but always stressin' about something."

"I'm just not hungry." She said.

"Awww leave my baby alone." Becka walked over with a plate full of food rubbing on Bari's back. "My baby just goin' through some growing pains."

I kissed Becka on the cheek and walked off. "Yeah... okay."

Sue and Tuff were at the kitchen counter sitting at the barstools looking like they were all extra in love and shit until I walked over.

"Heard you tryna hustle my man outta some money Gu." She chuckled.

Tuff simply looked at me and shrugged his shoulders.

I furrowed my brows to try to keep from laughing. "I ain't initiate that shit... don't believe the hype Sue."

Changing the subject, Tuff asked me about Qui. "So where this new girlfriend I keep hearing about? Seem like everybody met her but me."

"She's the one that let you in the house..." I said.

"What?!" he asked looking back. "Nah man, you aint got enough game to pull something as good looking as that."

"Watch ya'self Tuff." Sue warned.

"I didn't mean it like that baby..." he said laughing.

The mention of Qui had me thinking about her, where the fuck was she? At least ten minutes had gone buy and I hadn't seen her. I told her to unlock the door for Tuff and don't got too far and her ass did the opposite and came up missing. I walked off to go find her, only place she could be in the house was the bathroom so I knocked on the door.

"Someone is in here." She said from the other side of the door not sounding like herself at all.

"Lil mama... you aiight?" I asked her. "You been missin' for a lil minute, I was just checkin' on you."

The door immediately swung open upon her hearing my voice. She looked flushed and stressed in the face as she pulled me in and locked the door back before sitting on the lid of the toilet with her face in her palms. For the next ten seconds I just stood there in silence before I said anything.

"What happened Qui?" I asked. "You remember something else?" I questioned her past aware that at this point anything could possibly come back to her little by little and cause her to have one of the moments that she was having now.

She shook her head and sighed. "Gu I have something to tell you and I really hope that this wont change or relationship."

Now she was getting' me mad tight... like if this muhfucka was bout to tell me she had HIV or some off the wall shit... or even if she was about to tell me she cheated on me... I was gonna break her fuckin' neck. "Get it out lil mama... since when you can't talk to me?"

"I lied..." she said looking in my face for an reaction.

"You wanna share with me the details of what the fuck you talkin' bout Qui?" I felt the anger boiling inside of me wondering what the fuck she could've possibly lied about.

She took a deep breath, "Gu... I know who killed your cousin."

My fucking heart dropped and before I knew it, I saw red. I wanted to choke slam her ass for lying to me but I had to refrain myself. "Who killed Ronnie?" I asked through gritted teeth.

The tears were falling down her eyes, which I knew was coming cause she was sensitive as fuck anyway... but what I didn't expect were the words that came outta her mouth next... "the man who just walked in this house killed Ronnie..."

Mannnn I nearly kicked a whole in the fucking wall. Now I was all up in lil mama's face squeezing her by the arms ignoring the fear in her eyes. "Tuff?" I asked with wild eyes. "Yo lil mama... I'ma ask you this one time and one time only before I go blow this muhfuckas head off... are-you-fuckin'-sure?!"

She nod her head 'yes'.... "I'm sure." She sniffed and I knew she wasn't lying.

I pulled my gun from the small of my back... "I'ma kill this snake ass muhfucka!" I went to unlock the door.

"No! Gu wait!" Qui hopped up grabbing me using all her strength to pull me back.

I snatched away from her, "for what?! I need to handle this muhfucka now!"

"But that's not it!" She blurted while searching my eyes through her own tears.

I didn't know how much more I could take... "what the fuck else Qui?!"

She looked at me with sympathetic eyes and immediately I felt a dagger in my heart before she even said some shit I'd never thought would be coming outta her mouth.... "And Bari was there...."

I could've passed the fuck out....

To Be Continued....

Thank You

I'd like to thank each and every one of you that took the time out to read the first installment of this series. I hope you've grown to love and feel some kind of connection with these characters just as I did writing about them. Often times we ignore the real life situations happening around us without acknowledging the fact that these type of things are really happening in real life... someone somewhere is able to relate to each and every character in this book and my goal was to bring out the realness in those situations. I truly hope I've exceeded your expectations with the craft of work in this book. This has been one of my best pieces of work thus far and I can't wait to give you all the next installment to see how it all plays out and answer any questions that you may have... please feel free to follow me on social media... and also feel free to join my mailing list by simply texting ShalainePresents to 22828 and reply with your email. I love to stay connected with my readers and hear your thoughts and inputs. Please review the next page for my contact information.

Contact Information

Facebook: Shalaine Yvonne Powell
Facebook: Authoress S.Yvonne
Instagram: Authoress_s.yvonne
Email: Shalaine_presents@yahoo.com

I do reply to all emails within' 24 hours so please don't be reserved about reaching out. Also... don't forget to leave your review... and again, thank you.

-S.Yvonne

CPSIA information can be obtained
at www.ICGtesting.com
Printed in the USA
LVOW10s2335190118
563260LV00021B/805/P